Retaliation
Earth Reclamation Force

Martin Wallace

ISBN 9780957501539

2nd Edition

DEDICATION

To my beautiful daughters Isobel and Sophia, you both inspire me daily to achieve greatness. To my amazing wife Lyndsey, your strength and support is what allowed me to complete this book and move forward with living my dream. Thank you so much I love you all.

Preface

The date is the 22nd December 2018, my name is Lt Commander Scott Cave. On my first day at Navy flight school it turned out there were three Scott's in the class so I have been known as SC ever since. I am a helicopter pilot; however these days I fly something a bit different, a small one person fighter craft called a Fire-starter. Where do I fly it? That would be outer space.

In the year 2000 everyone waited for the world to come crashing down, for the computers to give up and life as we knew it to end. It didn't, but what did happen was the beginning of the end. The US government made the decision to militarize space and they started launching shuttles in secret, destination: the Moon. These weren't any normal shuttles, they had more powerful engines than anyone had seen before, making the journey take hours rather than days. These craft carried all the supplies required to build a structure on the rocky surface, but this was no small building, instead it was a large domed design with arms feeding off to a number of other glass environmental hubs designed to support life and everything that people may need to survive; then out of the rock they dug a massive hole and erected a metal roof over the top and sealed it with hydraulic vacuum doors, forming the first space based shipyard.

The legendary Area 51 had been the original home for the United States Space Force (USSF), but now they had plans for a much larger type of ship so big that it couldn't take off unnoticed from Earth. Construction began in the new facility and by the end of 2003 the USSF not only had their Moon base but the first Space Cruiser that could travel to other systems. The USSF kept building more and more ships, sending them off to the stars with one goal, finding other species and technology: weaponry, engines, communications, medicine and equipment and bring them back to Earth.

It took a while before they found anybody or anything, based on the fact that Space is a vast and desolate place and when they did find other species, they weren't always willing to trade. However, with a growing budget and little to show for it, the USSF would take what they couldn't trade for- in a lot of cases by force. This did not give them a good reputation throughout the galaxy and attracted unwanted attention. Despite their actions they were starting to yield bigger and better prizes, with the weaponry and engines being kept for the USSF and all other finds were funnelled through Fortune 500 companies to be reverse engineered and released to the unsuspecting public as technological breakthroughs. Most of the advanced products of the last ten years have come through the USSFs exploits in space. The technology the USSF was using had improved also, with a flight to the moon now taking minutes as opposed to hours and a flight to Mars would be well under an hour.

Everything in our little part of the universe was becoming more advanced.

By the end of 2007 the traffic coming and going from the moon had become too much and risked detection from star spotters, so a new base of operations was built on Mars which would be even bigger and better than the Moon. By the middle of 2009 all USSF operations were running out of the Mars base making the Moon facility obsolete, so it was powered down and a skeleton staff left in place to monitor it. At the end of 2016 the USSF had more than thirty ships of all different classifications, including Destroyers, which were smaller more agile craft, Frigates that were medium sized power houses, Cruisers that were palatial ships akin to flying cities with massive crews built to give and take a beating such as the old naval battleships. Unlike the Naval craft however they weren't really built to be in the thick of combat but instead to ensure the safe transport of fighter craft into battle. The USSF had amassed such an armada that nothing scared them, in their travels they had not encountered any species that could really challenge their military might and their arrogance became too much. The world below, however, still knew nothing of space exploration, other life forms or the unrelenting theft from throughout the galaxy.

On the 28th July 2017 they came; their name, the Fedirian's. Of course I, like most others on Earth, found that out later as they didn't really stop to introduce themselves. It would appear that these were one of the species to whom the USSF had caught the attention of and they were fierce, a cancerous war loving race with technology superior to our own. The battle was quick and brutal. I say battle as it certainly didn't last long enough for a war. They arrived

3

with twice the amount of ships that Earth owned and they shot on sight, thousands of fighters accompanied by heavily armed gunships poured onto the planet, whilst Cruisers and destroyers made short work of our mighty space army. The USSF was left in tatters; two thirds of their fleet destroyed, the other third fleeing for safety, leaving almost everyone on Earth behind. On the ground we fared no better: there was no warning, no siren, before anybody knew what was going on they were on top of us. They took out our airfields, destroying our active jets before they got off of the ground; troops, tanks and other ground based forces were destroyed from the air with little effort. The decision was made by the combined governments, or what was left of them, to launch nuclear weapons at the invading craft, such as the gunships and a Cruiser that had descended into the atmosphere. Although causing some damage to the invaders and destroying some ships, they killed the planet; it was doubtful that anyone would survive the radiation, radiation that would make a large part of the planet, if not all of it, uninhabitable for a thousand years. The only fighting that had been in anyway effective up to this point was sea-to-air combat with the enemy fighters.

I was aboard the HMS Edinburgh, a type 42 Royal Naval Destroyer, my role was as a helicopter pilot transporting people and supplies from between ships and the mainland. We had survived an encounter with a squadron of enemy fighters and were deep in the process of conducting repairs, although we knew all hope of survival was gone: once the radiation hit us we would be condemned to die along with everyone in the target zones, but the decision was made to fight until the end. This was until a small shuttle crash landed in the water close to our ship. It was not a design we recognised, but the Stars and Stripes on the side let us know that it was of human origin. The shuttle was secured to the side of our ship and the pilot treated for his injuries; his name was Commander Paul Riley, the Cruiser he was assigned to had been destroyed and he and some others had escaped in shuttles. Unfortunately, as his craft was last one out of the hangar bay, the shuttle was damaged in the explosion. He explained that if he could get the ship airborne again, we could escape to the base on the moon as it was believed to still be active. Given a choice of certain death or possible salvation my crew and I quickly got to work on his shuttle, taking around half a day to repair it. Once the ship was ready we said goodbye to the Edinburgh and took flight for our new home.

The Mars base had been completely destroyed during the opening attack, but as the facility on the Moon had been powered down it went completely unnoticed by the Fedirian's, allowing small shuttles such as ours to sneak in undetected and live under their noses. Riley, amongst others, slipped back in to Earth a few times in the weeks that followed in an attempt to collect survivors; those rescued were found predominately on Naval Vessels in areas not yet effected by radiation. Within one month we had around six thousand people living in secret on the moon.

The Fedirian's stuck around Earth like an occupying force; though unable to land or utilise the planet themselves, they seemed unwilling to move on, leaving the surviving members of the human race resigned to a life in hiding. During our exile on the Moon we discovered that the base contained a working ship yard along with the specifications and materials to build all manner of ships. We had to hand it to the US Military: they don't do anything by half. It was a wise assumption that living secretly on the moon long term was perhaps not a viable option, so a new strategy had to be found. Being careful not to attract unwanted attention the ship yard was re-activated and, with the assistance of a USSF technician by the name of Haver, plans were altered to accommodate more space for living quarters and the automated processes began building destroyers, frigates, carriers and small fighter craft called Fire-starters. The ship yard was efficient and it did not take long to produce a fleet large enough to house everyone in the base, although like the USSF before us for some reason we didn't just stop building; as was always the problem with opting for a military leadership, they always want more.

I'll never know if we had stopped building ships would that have made a difference, but we didn't and they found us: five months after the initial attack on Earth, here we were again under attack by the same species. Just like before the attack was a complete surprise, the only difference being that this time we had been expecting that an attack could happen so we all reacted well. We fought our way out of the solar system and despite losing some more people as we went, as a race we survived, all disappearing into the vastness of space to reconvene at a specified rendezvous point later as soon as we were sure we hadn't been followed. It's amazing how nearly becoming extinct can make you prepared and paranoid at the same time.

Once we rendezvoused it was time to take stock, out of around six thousand people on the moon just a little over four thousand five hundred remained, spread out between one carrier, one frigate and three destroyers. The fleet also held around sixty Fire-starters and a couple of scout shuttles: this was to be the beginning of the ERF: Earth Reclamation Force.

If there were other humans out there we would find them, if there was another place we could call home we would colonise it and, although our world might be gone, we would avenge those who were no longer with us, reclaiming everything we could that humanity had lost and this is our story.

Chapter 1

1 year later:

'Bank left and try and get round behind him, I'll draw his fire and you shut him down,' commanded SC through his comm system, sweat dripping down his face. Despite being in a climate controlled cabin the heat of battle made the Flight Commander flushed. Lt Smeaton immediately responded and carried out the tactical manoeuvre, bringing his Fire-starter in behind the enemy fighter craft. SC violently twisted and turned his little craft, affectionately named Speedy, avoiding the plasma fire of the enemy ship, allowing Smeaton to gain position and open fire, hitting the craft at point blank range and causing it to explode in a mass of fire-works.

'Good work, Lt.' Bellowed SC down the comm.

'Thanks, Commander. That was a close one'

'Tell me about it, that's the fourth strike in 3 days, the Feds have really stepped up their game. We better get back to the Swan and report in.'

'Copy that Sir'

For all the negativity that had befallen him, SC was amazed at his current role. Although he was used to serving in the military, it was how he was serving that impressed him the most: 17 months ago he had been a helicopter pilot flying between naval ships, an airborne taxi driver, transporting officers and soldiers around and now here he was, a top space fighter pilot in charge of a squadron of novices, fighting against the most dangerous species in the galaxy. 'Life is like a movie these days,' he thought to himself.

The Swan was a small tactical destroyer, its appearance white in colour, large engine mounts sweep up at a 45 degree angle to the rear of the ship, giving it the look of a winged bird, being one of the main reasons for its name. The construction of its hull was a reinforced armour, at least four times as thick as on the Fire Starter fighter craft. The Swan had two large rail guns on the front of the ship and a number of chain guns installed tactically around her body and rear. Destroyers such as the Swan serve as scout crafts for investigating new areas or as support vessels for the larger fleet in conflicts. A squadron of eight Fire-starters accompanied the destroyer and provide fighter support in case of attack. These fighters were small and manoeuvrable and contain forward facing chain guns; their light armour provided a vulnerability, which meant that pilots must avoid enemy fire at all costs. When not in use the fighters were normally housed within the Swan's small landing bay, allowing them to travel with the larger craft at the faster than light speeds it needed to move between star systems.

SC followed Smeaton into the landing bay, allowing the less experienced pilot to touch down before proceeding to throttle back and negotiate the tight entrance into the ship's hangar, joining the fighters from the rest of the squadron. He exited the craft and directed Smeaton to gather the pilots in the briefing room, as there would be an update after he had checked in with command.

SC took the familiar route to the command deck to report in person to the ship's Captain what had taken place. Climbing the three floors and walking steadily along the straight corridor to the command deck had given SC time to consider the events so far; it had been a quiet morning on board the Swan when the alert sounded that enemy fighters were incoming. He and Smeaton had scrambled to their fighters and intercepted the two Fedirian craft. The purpose of the Swans' trip to this sector was to scout out the area for energy resources, which after a year of the fleet being marooned in space were becoming increasingly short. The fact that they were discovered by Fedirian forces four times in three days didn't bode well for this being a safe sector for mining, no matter what value it held, which at this point SC was pretty sure was none, as in the three days that they had been in this system they had yet to find anything useful.

SC walked on to the command deck; it was a vast yet efficient space with computers on three walls and a large viewing Screen on the fourth. The deck was busy with approximately twenty people scuttling around busily doing things. To the untrained eye, it wasn't apparent what anybody was doing, but SC was more than aware of the complexities of running a ship. As much as SC enjoyed the one on one combat element of the Fire Starters, he looked forward to the challenge of commanding a large ship such as this one day. A ship with the power to effect serious change in any conflict, where everyone on board is relying on you to make the right decisions.

'Lt Commander, it's good to see you alive!' bellowed SCs commanding officer from across the deck. He turned to see her walking toward him, a blonde woman standing average height with soft attractive features, owning the look of a woman ten years her junior and she was wearing a warm smile that he knew to be genuine.

'Hi Selina, it's good to see you too.'

'That's Captain Laverty to you!'

'Of course, my mistake, apologise Captain,' smirked SC; he had known Selina Laverty as an officer in the Navy, he requested the assignment to her ship when she was given command. It was good to work beside someone he knew he could trust. 'I thought you would like my report, Captain!' Placing emphasis on the last word for effect.

'Thank-you, Commander, that would be swell.'

'Lt Smeaton and I engaged two enemy fighters on the other side of the moon, I was able to destroy the first one during the initial pass, then I acted as a decoy allowing Smeaton to gain position and destroy the second. The engagement lasted less than two minutes start to finish.'

'Could you tell what they were doing there? Were they looking for us?'

'I can't tell you for certain if they were looking for something or not; however, my opinion would be that they seemed to be on a standard sweeping search pattern. It might be a standard patrol zone, I doubt they were able to let anyone know we were here, we got the drop on them and it was over before they knew it. It was lucky we picked them up on sensors before they detected us. Can I have permission to take out my squad to do some recon and see if we can find what, if anything, they were searching for?'

'I wish you could but we have been sent new orders, I need you to brief your pilots.'

'Road trip?' the Flight Commander responded smiling, 'are we going anywhere fun?'

'Instead of mining we are going thieving,' replied the Captain.

SC rolled his eyes, 'Can I ask what we are thieving and who it is from?'

'Apparently there is a weapons cache on board a Fedirian space station in the Tango system; however, our information tells us that the facility is all but abandoned and has minimal security. Our orders are to head there directly, disable any automated defences and remaining fighter craft, dock with the station and take any and all useful weapons and equipment,' reported Laverty.

'Sounds like fun, I didn't hear a lot of we in that sentence, am I to assume we won't be joining up with the fleet for the attack?' Inquired the pilot.

'No, sorry, it's just us I'm afraid.'

SC gave his Captain a look of frustration. 'Look Selina, I trust you, but what are we getting into here? What info do we have? Numbers of defending units, the armament of the station?'

'These are our orders, Commander,' Selina scolded, 'we have limited information on the defences of the station and limited time for the operation, I have been assured that the resistance should be light. Now I need you to do your job and brief your pilots and support this ship as it goes into battle.'

'I understand! Oh and Captain, you don't have to give me the hard line, you know I'll do anything for you, I just don't like walking into situations when I don't have any facts. Can I ask when we are departing?'

'Straight away. The brass want these weapons badly and we are the closest ship, so we need to be ready for attack in about three hours.'

'Just out of idle curiosity, is there is no one nearby who could back us up?' Asked SC hopefully.

'I have sent a request for assistance; however, apparently this is the best window for the raid and no other ship is likely to make it on time. So we will have to go it alone and hope for the best.'

'It's that word "hope" that fills me with dread,' replied SC as he turned and walked away.

Selina looked at him muttering under her breath, 'Me too,' as she detected a sick feeling in the pit of her stomach.

The pilots briefing lounge is just like a large classroom with a smart board at the front, a lecture podium and rows of fixed leather chairs. All seven squadron pilots were there waiting for their squadron leader; they are the Dark Knights, possibly a more impressive title than group. SC picked it to encourage morale; if they sounded cool then they would be cool, however the majority of the fleet was manned by novices who didn't have a military background, and the Knights were no different. They were made up of Smeaton, a slightly rotund man in his late twenties, possibly the best natural pilot of the novices; he had a private flying licence prior to the abandoning of Earth. Lt Ward, second in command of the Knights, was an attractive and intelligent pilot who takes charge of discipline amongst the others: Former Navy personnel who worked with SC, and was the only pilot next to SC who wasn't a novice. Whyte was a former commercial airline pilot, probably had the hardest time getting used to flying such small craft, but has shown vast improvement in recent missions. Santora, Marks, Whiterod and Karran make up the rest of the Dark Knight squadron, a range of young pilots from a variety of areas, from Marks-a former crop duster-to Whiterod, a stunt pilot. Over the last four months SC has been attempting to turn them into a crack unit that would benefit any campaign and accomplish his primary goal, which was getting each of them back alive.

Standing at his podium at the front of the room, the flight Commander looked at the relatively jovial group of pilots. 'Ok people, it's go time, the ship will be getting underway soon to take us to the Tango system, where we will all be seeing some action; we don't know quite what we are in for but the fun begins in around three hours, all I can really say is that the Ship is hitting a Fedirian space station. This is a drive by with a smash and grab, it'll be our job to clear all defences with the assistance of the Swan, then cover and assist whilst they link up and grab what we are there for: the operation should take no more than 30 minutes. Any questions?' SC felt that the best way of delivering news like this was matter-of-factly. Whether or not he agreed with the mission was irrelevant: he had to make sure his people knew that there was no room for negotiation.

The first volley came from Ward, 'What are we there for?'

'Weapons, a cache that's been left under soft guard,' replied the lead pilot.

'How soft?' asked Santora. Originally of Indian descent, she was an attractive woman with flowing black hair and an athletic build; she spoke perfect English as a result of being born in the UK.

'We don't know, intelligence says a few fighters and station defences, but the opinion is we should be able to handle it.'

'Do I take it from that, we aren't expecting any backup?' voiced the deceptively mousey Karran. A red-haired twenty something who appeared as though she could be scared of her own shadow, but when given the chance was as vocal as anyone SC had ever met.

'Can't count on it, no other ships are close enough so we have to assume it's just us.' SC took a breath and looked at the solemn faces and spoke, 'we will go through the tactical plan and everyone will know what to do, we will ensure that we make this as easy as possible. We will survive this.'

'Yes sir!' responded SC's Knights.

Chapter 2

The Swan completed its overdrive jump into the Tango system and once in position they hid themselves behind a moon just out of scanner range of the Fedirian space station.

Captain Laverty gave the green light to her command crew to prepare for the attack. Leaning into the comm system she spoke softly with a trace of hope in her voice, 'All Fire-starters are go for launch, good luck pilots.'

At which point the eight fighter craft began deploying from the ship, quickly adjusting their position and forming up alongside the Swan, four Fire starters on each side they awaited instructions to proceed into battle.

'All Fire-starters accounted for and ready to go, Captain!' reported SC through his comm unit.

'Thank you Commander, proceed with the plan now. Good hunting,' replied Selina.

'Will do Captain.'

The agreed attack plan had the Swan and her escort move out in formation with a strategically planned simultaneous strike on any fighter craft and the weapons systems of the space station, the idea being that the moment the enemy noticed the incoming force, they were exploding in a hail of weapons fire, which in theory would lead to a quick and concise victory.

The attack force negotiated their way around the moon, keeping as close as possible to its electromagnetic field, allowing the moon to mask their approach from the enemy sensors for as long as possible, assisting with the element of surprise. As the Swan and her fighters emerged from the protection of the moon they were in weapons range and in one simultaneous burst they let their weapons go free.

The Swan itself concentrated it's fire on one of the space stations eight plasma canons; after making short work of the first one they moved on to the second. There were six enemy fighter craft surrounding the space station; these were instantly destroyed by Ward, Smeaton, Marks, Whiterod, Santora, and Whyte. SC and Karran directed their attack on the station's plasma weapons, taking out one in the first hit by themselves and then combined with the rest of the squadron to attack the second. The Swan absorbed some hits from the station whilst it took out a third and then a fourth plasma weapon. The remainder of the Knights had adjusted their targets to the remaining plasma guns of the station and proceeded to destroy them with minimum difficulty.

In the space of 5 minutes the attack force had succeeded in the first stage of their plan, with all of the enemy fighters destroyed and the space station tactically disabled: this supported the theory that the intelligence was correct and that this would be an easy assault on a soft target, more than able to be handled by one ship.

Selina breathed a sigh of relief as the last plasma weapons were destroyed. 'Well done Commander,' the Captain announced through her comm unit.

'Thank you Captain, we will cover your back now, whilst you get what we came for,' replied the young pilot, who couldn't help but be suspicious that the victory was easier than it should have been.

'Thank you Commander, we are moving in to dock now. Stay on station and we will be finished soon.'

Selina turned to her second in command, 'Commander Hill, prepare your tactical team to lead the raid on the station, I want to us to locate the weapon cache and have it loaded and be ready to leave within the hour.'

'Aye Captain, we will be ready to go as soon as the ship is docked,' replied the former Army soldier.

'Very good, Commander.'

The Swan took position alongside the obviously aging Space Station, the battered nature of the armoured hull meant that it took a few minutes to secure a tight connection with the docking hatch, although soon enough they were securely on station prepared to deploy the tactical team.

'We have compression with the airlock, tactical team ready to disembark,' reported Hill

'Good luck Commander Hill. Be quick and keep alert, we don't know what you're heading into,' warned Laverty.

The hatch onto the Space Station slid open with ease; this was strange in itself as they had expected to have to forcibly gain access with explosives. Immediately, the tactical team took cover expecting to come under defensive fire, positioning themselves against the side of the ship so they would be protected by the bulkhead. But nothing came. Slowly and strategically the team moved down the long metallic corridor, keeping continuous watch, awaiting the sudden appearance of enemy soldiers. Commander Hill moved though the ship like a Panther stalking prey, demonstrating the seasoned expert he was. Previously a sergeant in the US Army, he was used to leading soldiers into battle, but nothing prepared him for the calm and quiet of this space station. Stationed in Afghanistan and Iraq for multiple tours, he had become accustomed to hostile situations and not knowing what to expect; however the one thing he was always sure of, was if something seemed too good to be true, then it most likely was.

'Why is there no one shooting at us, it doesn't make sense.' he said to no one in particular.

Following close behind Hill was Sergeant Pillar, 'With all due respect, Sir, it's kinda nice not being shot at.'

'This is too suspicious, at least you know where you are when people are shooting at you,' replied the gruff soldier.

Posting guards along the way to protect the return passage the team made good progress on their way to the storage area containing the weapons. An accurate layout of the station had been provided by command, which made a pleasant change from normal. Luckily the storage area where they were heading wasn't far from the airlock where they entered.

The storage room was filled with boxes and crates, most appearing like they were full of repackaged parts. Upon inspection the boxes appeared to contain a range of hand plasma weapons and the parts to construct ship mounted plasma canons, which would likely be a massive improvement on the chain guns equipped on most of the ERF's vessels.

'This is what we came for, start moving this stuff back to the ship and keep your eyes open; it's still too quiet,' ordered the Commander to his remaining troops.

Outside the space station it turned out that Hill wasn't the only one worried about the silence, SC and his Knights had setup a sweeping patrol of the area surrounding the Space Station watching out for any incoming craft. 'This quiet is making me uneasy.' whispered the senior pilot.

'Commander, I feel like you want this to go wrong,' observed Karran, 'Personally, I am enjoying the quiet. I say lots more quiet, and keep it coming.'

'It's been too easy, I would love it to be this easy but it just seems unlikely, I mean they barely got off a shot before we disabled them and now there is no welcoming committee on the station. It just seems wrong and that's a fact. This is not a feeling I will shake until we are safely out of this system and heading back to the fleet,' responded the wary pilot.

'Just don't jinx us Sir, I want to get home from this.' laughed Karran.

Just then SC's comm crackled, 'Commander, the tactical team is just loading the last of the weapons onto the ship now, we will be underway in ten minutes,' Selina reported.

'Copy that Captain, the sooner the better,' responded SC.

Selina Laverty smiled as she replied, 'I'm right there with you on that, we will be heading off so... Wait hold on.'

The Captain studied her view screen as she waited for confirmation of the readings on the console in front of her.

'Captain what's going on?' Shouted SC.

'Detach, detach now!' barked the Captain to Parsons, the helmsman.

'Selina, what's happening?' Demanded the Fire-starter Commander.

SC looked round to see the Space Station starting to explode from the central pod and detonations moving out to the docking arms. The Swan had started moving away but then became engulfed in the flames.

'Selina!' SC cried out in helpless despair.

Just then Wards' voice came through on the comm, 'Commander, incoming contacts, we have fighters and heavies in-bound.'

Appearing into the system from all around the Fire-starters were enemy fighter craft, numbering around fifty along with two large Fedirian destroyers.

Through the comm unit a voice broke gently, 'SC.'

'Selina is that you?'

'Yes, we are ok, a bit damaged and worse for wear, but the armour held up.' the Captain replied.

'You need to get the Swan out of here, you are in no shape for a fight at the moment; we can cover you if you retreat now.' requested the Lt Commander.

'Sorry Commande,r but that's not going to work, I'm in charge and we will not leave you to die here. All hands to battle stations, Fire-starters engage those fighters we will hold off the destroyers.' barked Selina.

'Captain, I must protest, there is no way you can take both of them.' answered SC.

'Then we will take as many of them as we can,' replied the defiant Captain.

SC knew that surviving this conflict would be a long shot, but he was damned if he was going to let Selina and the Swan die without a fight, 'Knights engage fighters, try to draw them all away from the Swan, stick with your wingman and watch your ass, good hunting.'

'I knew you would screw this up for me.' replied Karran. SC couldn't help but smile at the badly timed remark.

The Dark Knights moved out in the four directions in an attempt to keep all enemy fighters away from the injured command ship. Selina Laverty positioned the Swan to engage one of the two destroyers attempting to take out their plasma cannons and reduce the impact of the firepower on her damaged ship; although a good strategy, this was an unrealistic expectation as the second destroyer was free to hammer the Swans defences without distraction, and that is exactly what it did.

SC's Knights quickly engaged the enemy and their considerable training was paying off, allowing them to avoid fire by weaving their craft whilst destroying enemy fighters. For a moment the knights seemed indestructible, SC was feeling so much pride in his pilots until they were served a rude awakening. Marks the crop duster fell into the sights of one Fedirian fighter, letting rip his small plasma canons he reduced the craft to a ball of flames. Marks wingman Smeaton could be heard screaming over the comm system in shock, distraught at the loss of his comrade. All the pilots felt the loss, this was the first loss of the team since they were put together 12 months before, but this was no time for grieving as they knew that one false move could have them all in the same position.

SC had clocked up his sixth kill, but could not ignore the fact that Marks was more than likely to be the first of the losses due to the thirty to forty enemy craft still in the air, he then turned his attention to the Swan that was taking a beating which could not be sustained. The Swan had made some progress in disabling one of the Destroyers' three plasma cannons and was hard at work on the second; however, the second Destroyer was still firing all three cannons at Selina's ship, the ERF ships' manoeuvrability meaning that not all ships were hitting home, but enough so that damage was being done. 'Naomi you and the remaining knights continue the assault on the fighters, Karran you're with me, we are going to engage that second destroyer.'

Naomi Ward nodded to herself, 'Yes Commander, but you be careful, that thing will make short work of you if it hits you.'

'I better make sure I don't get hit then,' replied SC.

'Yeah but what about me,' smirked Karran, 'I knew being your wingman would get me killed.'

Sally Karran was a personal pilot licence holder; before the attack on Earth, she had been forced to land her small plane on a deserted runway when the sky had become filled with enemy fighters. That same runway became an emergency landing point for Army troop carriers, which had lost the battlefield and been forced into retreat. Karran encountered Hill and his team and it was from there that they were picked up by Riley on one of his clandestine flights back to the planet. She was sure she was as good as dead until that pick up, never had she been so sure, until maybe now when her and her crazy Commander were going to engage a ship at least thirty times their size.

SC and his wingman took up an attack position on the much larger craft, targeting the destroyer's weapons, hoping to attract the attention away from the Swan which was looking like it was about to fall apart. The plan worked and the second destroyer started focusing its firepower on the two annoying Fire Starters which were hammering their plasma guns. However, this may have been too little too late, as the Swan was in a bad way. SC and Karran were bobbing and weaving their crafts much like a boxer in the ring trying to avoid being hit, and although they were taking the attention away from the Swan their weapons were making little impact on the enemy destroyer. It became evident that without a miracle the battle would be lost and they would not live to see the outcome.

'This is Captain Laverty to all hands, it's been a pleasure serving with you all. But I'm afraid we are about to lose structural integrity and the ship will be lost, prepare to abandon ship!'

'That's it! Sally fall back I'm going to ram this destroyer.' bellowed SC, having had enough he knew there was no chance of survival, but if he could take out the destroyer then just maybe the remaining Fire-starters could subdue the remaining fighters and give the rest of them a chance to survive.

'That's suicide sir, I can't let you do it.' replied the reluctant wingman.

'No choice, we cannot lose the Swan and this is the only chance we have of turning the tide,' responded SC as he set his small fighter craft on a collision course with the enemy vessel's command deck. Sally Karran backed her ship off, giving her wingman covering fire, selfishly she felt, at least with SC alive she stood a chance of survival; now she wasn't so sure at all.

Suddenly Ward's voice broke though the comm, 'Commander there is another contact incoming.'

'We can't take anymore.' SC saw his last ditch effort being worthless if another ship was to enter the fray; however, he maintained his approach whilst he awaited confirmation.

'It's the O'Neil,' shouted Ward.

'Paul you are a sight for sore eyes!' laughed SC into his comm, taking care to pull his craft out of its suicidal trajectory.

'Thought you might need some assistance, how can I help?' Remarked his old friend.

'The Swan is in trouble, can you take out that destroyer and then help me with this other one,' insisted the Lt Commander.

'No problem, I am dispatching a squadron of Fire Starters to assist with those enemy fighters as well,' stated Riley.

The O'Neil was a Tactical Destroyer commanded by Captain Paul Riley, SC's friend who rescued him off of the HMS Edinburgh seventeen months earlier. Riley's experience in the USSC meant that very quickly he was promoted to Captain and put in charge of one of the ERF's strongest and most powerful ships. The O'Neil had three rail guns on the front along with a wide array of chain guns flourishing its body, making it a formidable craft. Inside the ship contained two squadrons of Fire-starters, enabling it to provide comprehensive tactical support in any encounter.

The O'Neil's rail guns made short work of the first destroyer and allowed it to then concentrate its efforts on the second Destroyer's engines, which still had SC and Karran attacking its weapons. The Swan was doing its best to limp away from the battle under the cover of the O'Neil's Fire Starters as they couldn't take the risk of another blow.

Eventually the O'Neil and it's Fire Starters, along with the Dark Knights, were successful in defeating the Fedirian forces, happily without the loss of another craft. The Swan had sustained considerable damage but was still flying, although barely. However, not all of its crew were quite as lucky.

'What's the casualty count?' asked Captain Laverty.

'22 crewman and 1 pilot' answered Lt Haver, the Swan's Operations Officer.

'Out of a crew of only 120...I hope the weapons we came for are worth the sacrifice.' exclaimed the Captain.

After landing in the hangar bay SC quickly made his way to the command and control Centre to check on his Captain, finding himself running down the corridor until he could see the attractive blonde haired woman standing ahead of him. She looked a little fried and dishevelled but otherwise in one piece 'Hey Selina, are you hurt?' he called to her.

'No, I'm ok, just a couple of cuts and bruises, could have been much worse,' she replied.

'If Paul hadn't shown up I think we were all done for,' stated SC.

The Captain nodded her head in agreement, 'No argument from me.'

'Don't thank me, pay me!' bellowed Captain Paul Riley in his usual larger than life way from down the corridor.

'Paul good buddy, your timing is impeccable as ever, although earlier would have been better,' declared the Dark Knights Commander. 'However I have to ask, what were you doing here at all?'

'We got the call to do this raid initially then they called us back and we were told to stand down as you were closer, so we asked permission to join up with you and launch it as joint venture, but we were told that it couldn't wait and we should stand down and leave you to it. But you know me, I can't resist a good fight, so we pushed the engines to get here as quickly as we could. Just wish we could have gotten here a bit sooner,' answered the former USSF Captain.

'No regrets on that one, we are happy you turned up at all,' responded Selina.

'To be honest, a moment later and there wouldn't have been anything left to save,' interjected SC.

'So what was it that you were stealing that was so time sensitive?' Asked Paul.

'Plasma weapons it would seem, that's it as far as we can see.' answered Selina. 'But nobody expected the place to go boom, especially not whilst we were still attached.'

SC coughed.

All eyes turned to look at him; after a moments awkward silence it was Selina who spoke, 'Go on then, speak.'

'Captains, far be it from me as a lowly Lt Commander to suggest this through fear of Court Marshall, but is it at all possible that command knew about the self-destruct on board the station? Could it be that it was timed to go off at a certain point, and that's why they couldn't wait for us to join with the O'Neil?'

'But then why not tell us so we knew how much time we had?' asked Selina.

'If you knew you had less than 4 hours to get to this system from where you were, defeat a standing guard, dock, potentially fight off troops and then empty a weapons cache and depart. What would you tell them?' offered Paul.

'That it couldn't be done,' answered Selina, the situation sinking in as she really now starting to consider it as a possibility. The expression on the Captain's face was easy to read: she looked dejected, 'I can't believe that they would do that to us, wait though, Command couldn't have known about the Destroyers. Also why would the Feds destroy a plasma stock? None of it makes sense!'

The hurried footsteps of the Swan's second in command came stomping across the deck, 'Captain! I may be able to answer that question.'

'Commander Hill, what do you know?'

'I have been inspecting the weapons parts we collected from the station; it seems as though they are an older, possibly discontinued model, compared to the current weapons on board the Fedirian ships. In addition to that, after working with Lt Haver we have established that the station itself was also quite old and was in a decaying orbit. Day by day it was slowly heading towards the planet below, so as a security measure, rather than allow their technology to fall into enemy hands, they were destroying the station and their stockpile of outdated weaponry,' concluded the Commander.

'Where did the Destroyers come from?' inquired SC.

'It would appear, according to intercepted transmissions, that when we attacked the station there was an automated signal sent to the nearest Fedirian patrol, so they dispatched nearby security ships to investigate,' reported Hill.

'Does that mean there could be others on the way?' Inquired Captain Riley.

The Commander nodded, 'it would be wise to assume so, I would suggest we get the engines back online as soon as possible and vacate this system.'

'Thank you Commander,' answered Selina, 'Paul, would you mind hanging around for a little while and covering us whilst we make repairs?'

'No problem, we have the Zora sector to check out but it can wait until you're mobile,' smiled Riley.

The Captain returned the smile, 'OK thanks, we better get to work.'

Chapter 3

The Swan was badly damaged and despite the assistance from Captain Riley and the crew of the O'Neil, repairs were going slowly. The morale of the crew wasn't helping either: with around a fifth of the crew dead, there was a hole in the ship that nobody could repair. Most of the crew had been on board since fleeing the Moon base a year before and had become like a family. This was the biggest loss any of them had seen since the surprise attack.

Unfortunately this wasn't the time for mourning, as the ship was still in impending danger if they didn't leave the sector quickly. With this in mind the primary focus of repairs was the engines, which had taken a large amount of plasma fire during the battle. The next focus was weapons systems; if they couldn't run then they better be able to fight.

'Captain Laverty!'

'Yes, crewman.' Selina turned to see a young man in oil covered overalls saluting her, 'at ease.'

'The chief says that standard engines are fine for use, however overdrive is in bad shape, she can only get a short burst of power at the moment, but that's it until we can get back to the fleet and get some parts,' reported the engineer.

'How short a burst?' Inquired the Captain.

The young engineer's posture relaxed a little and with a look of discomfort on his face answered, 'Not likely to be more than two minutes.'

Selina stopped to consider for a moment before asking, 'Is that long enough to get us out of this system?'

'Yes, but we will burn out the overdrive and we will be restricted to our standard engines from then on,' replied the bewildered engineer.

'Which will leave us as sitting ducks if we are attacked.' Selina stated aloud to nobody in particular.

Although it wasn't necessary the engineer affirmed her point, 'Yes, Captain.'

'Thank you crewman, inform the Chief that we will be taking her up on her offer. However, I would appreciate each and every extra second she can give us.'

The engineer tensed up again and stood to attention before continuing, 'Understood, Captain.'

The crewman saluted and turned about, heading swiftly back towards the engine room. Selina turned towards the wall-mounted ship-wide communication unit and spoke sharply into it, 'SC report the Captain's office.'

The Captain's office had seen better days. Black char lines marked the walls, broken picture frames and furniture. The desk was in one piece though, 'Small comfort,' thought Selina as the chair for it was in pieces. She looked around thinking about how happy she had been when she was given command of such a fine ship, the one glimmer of good fortune in the dark storm they had all been living in for the past year or so. Her life had always been about the military, even as a young girl she was a sea cadet, then the navy, now the space force. Rules and order is what Selina Laverty knew, and for the most part enjoyed; she knew where she was with the military, that structure, that style, left little room for grey areas, but now she was realising that the very people she reported too and respected had nearly led her to her death. Had it been her choice, she may have still done it, but to be kept out of the loop wasn't sitting well with her. This wasn't the Charge of the Light Brigade; this was one of the few remaining pockets of the human race left in the galaxy. If it hadn't been for the O'Neil turning up when it did and SC's unrelenting support and defence of her and the Swan, she had no doubt that she wouldn't be here now.

'Ah SC,' she thought to herself. It made her feel better to have him around, that little bit of home, it was like being back on the HMS Edinburgh, how she missed those times they were so much simpler, but at least he was here now, with her, that person she could always count on to have her back and the only person she felt she could be her vulnerable self in front of, even if she didn't usually allow it.

The door beeped and then opened automatically. SC wasn't known to stand on ceremony and wait for an invitation to come in. He walked in looking tired with bags under his eyes, when he walked he was stiff as if his joints ached, yet still somehow heroic, tall and astute like nothing was phasing him and he could just take it all in his stride. Selina often wondered how he did that, was it just a front, a vale of confidence, or did nothing really get to him?

'What's happening, Captain? Are you redecorating? Because I have to say I liked it the way it was before.' he offered sarcastically.

'It's just something new I'm trying.' she joked back, 'Look, I've had word from the Chief, Overdrive is knackered and only good for a couple of minutes.'

SC nodded his head in acceptance of the news, 'Ah, right, I was hoping things hadn't hit rock bottom yet, turns out I was wrong. Is there nothing more the Chief can do?'

Selina shook her head, 'Not without parts, she's going to try to squeeze as much out of it as possible, it'll be enough to get us out of the system but that's about it. When the Feds get here and discover what has happened it likely won't take them long to find us.'

SC considered the situation, 'How long would it take to get back to the fleet if the Overdrive was working?'

'About 8 hours, give or take,' Selina estimated.

SC pondered her response, not looking forward to the reply to his next question, 'Without it?'

'About one week,' Selina frowned.

The news was no great surprise to SC. He held out hope that he may be pleasantly shocked, but that was not to be. 'So we really need as long as we can get at overdrive,' he mused, 'Ok then, we will need a rotation of security patrols keeping an eye out for enemy craft, also it may be an idea to send out a scout craft to find potential hiding places: nebulas, moons, asteroid fields, anything that we can use to escape detection.'

'We don't have a Scout craft on board so one of your Fire Starters will have to do it,' replied the Captain.

SC thought for a moment, 'I can send Ward, she is desperate to get out for a bit, she was close to Marks, being back on the ship is hard for her without him.'

'Ok then. We will set off in about 20 minutes,' responded the Captain, 'Just as soon as I get the word that the structural integrity will hold whilst we make the jump.'

'Makes sense,' replied SC, 'Best not hang around too long, I know we are moving on standard engines at the moment, but we aren't putting much space between us and them.'

'Amen to that,' affirmed the Captain.

SC reached out his hand and touched his Captains shoulder gently, 'you'll get us home Selina, I have faith in you.' Flashing her his warm smile combined with a sincere look. Selina touched his hand that was resting on her for a moment before they both brought themselves back to life.

SC turned around and headed for the door to prepare his team for the oncoming trials still to come, confident though that he was right: his Captain would get them home and he would help her however he could.

Selina found herself with the forming of tears in her eyes, she fought hard to hold them back before speaking, 'Commander.'

SC turned around to face his pretty blonde Captain, 'Yes.'

'Thank you.' she replied in a whispered tone.

'No problem, Captain.' SC smiled sincerely and turned away again.

As he walked away, the automatic door closed behind him, Selina stood with a single tear running down her face whist she thought, 'I only wish I could thank him properly.'

Twenty minutes later Selina was back on the Command deck of her ship, 'All hands prepare for overdrive!' Instructed Laverty.

Parsons the helmsman prepared his controls, 'Ready on your command Captain, engineering has confirmed they are good to go.'

'Engage, Mr. Parsons'

With that instruction given the damaged Swan leapt off into the darkness, moving at a speed faster than light. Bidding good-bye to the O'Neil, who was setting off on their own new mission. The ship hissed and clanked but seemed stable enough to hold together. Charting their progress the Captain, SC and Hill stood on the command deck, hoping for the miracle that would allow them to stay at this speed for a long time. This miracle was not to come and at after two minutes and thirty three seconds the overdrive engines died and the Swan resumed travelling at standard speed in normal space.

True to his word, SC dispatched Ward to Scout ahead and keep her eyes open for enemy craft or potential hiding places. There was a two Fire Starter patrol organised, rotating every four hours and providing covering support to the injured craft, ensuring that no one would come up on her unnoticed, so the ship and crew settled in for the long haul of a week-long crawl through open space.

After a day of travel, although tired and upset about the previous day's events, the crew began to settle and relax. No sign of the enemy in twenty four hours was making everyone think that they were out of the woods. They were, however, still a long way from the fleet and they were in no position to run or fight if they met enemy combatants. For any military people this had to be the worst situation to be in and the crew of the Swan were no different. The engineering team was still carrying out repairs, focusing on weapons and structural integrity. Progress was slow as they couldn't get outside to work on the areas they needed too and were restricted by the lack of available parts.

SC had ordered the escort craft to patrol from a distance, allowing them the opportunity to pick up the presence of enemy craft before they could detect the Swan. This turned out to be a fortunate tactic as on the second day Whiterod and Santora picked up a signal from a contact which was closing on their position, and although not rapidly, it was gaining on them. A signal was sent out and Ward was instantly called back from her scouting mission to reconvene with the ship in the closest available hiding place that she had identified.

The Swan took position behind a large moon in the current system, using the moon's radiation to mask detection, and creating a barrier for line of sight. The senior staff were called to Laverty's office for a quick strategy meeting. 'How long can we hide here?' questioned Commander Hill.

The Captain looked at her Operations chief, 'Mr Haver, what do you think?'

'Well Captain, providing they don't come too close to the Moon, then they would never find us, with any luck they may fly right past and never know we were here,' answered Haver confidently.

Hill rolled his eyes, 'When have we ever been that lucky?'

SC, looking puzzled, asked, 'How did they find us anyway? We have been on the move for nearly two days, there are a hundred different places we could be, are we honestly thinking this is random chance?'

'Seems unlikely.' voiced Laverty, 'What other explanations do we have? Ones that make more sense.' Everyone turned to look at Haver again, hoping he may have some more knowledge to impart.

Being the ships Operations Officer did make Haver a target for all technical questions. Normally he relished the attention of being the smartest guy in the room, but over the last few days, with the situation becoming increasingly desperate, it was a responsibility that was wearing on him. Still he knew he couldn't disappoint, and a plausible suggestion was thought out. 'It's possible that we are trailing plasma; our overdrive shut down mid-flow, it's not designed to just be switched on and off. Just shutting it off as we did could have created a leak.'

'Ok,' acknowledged the Captain nodding her head, 'that seems logical and makes more sense than random chance.'

SC nodded his head in agreement, 'If that's true and they are following that trail, they'll be on us soon, so we don't have much time, so no hope of them flying right past us.'

'Ok then, all-and I do mean all- of you, does anyone have any ideas of how we get out of this?' asked the Captain. Nobody made eye contact with the Captain straight away, it was obvious they were all thinking, but no one was really sure whether each other had an idea or were just looking for a way to avoid saying that they had nothing. Haver was starting to feel the pressure again, but he was coming up blank when, to his relief, he heard a voice.

The voice was that of SC, 'Well, I do have one really bad idea,' suddenly everyone was staring at him, 'We could attack them!'

Shocked and stunned looks appeared on all three faces simultaneously, all open mouthed and unsure how to respond, Hill looked incredulous, but it was the Captain who found her voice first, 'Are you mad? This ship barely survived her last entanglement with one of those destroyers and we do not have the O'Neil to bail us out this time, how could we possibly attack them?'

SC calmly returned Selina's look and continued, 'Running isn't an option, we have no speed, we can't play cat and mouse as there are not enough mouse holes to hide in, which only leaves fight; however, we may not need the O'Neil, also with what I have in mind, if it works, it could get us home a bit quicker, too.' Turning his attention to the young Operations Officer Haver, 'Our overdrive engines were developed from technology we picked up from another race, weren't they?'

The former USSF officer nodded in agreement, 'I believe they were called the Croats.'

'Good,' stated SC, 'If I remember what I was told correctly, then they are the same race that the Fedirian's used to improve their engine design. Meaning if I'm right, if we could disable their ship without destroying it, then we may be able to get the parts we need to fix the Swan's overdrive from them.'

'Brilliant SC,' the Captain replied sarcastically, 'just one slight issue, you still haven't told us how you intend disabling that ship.'

'Patience Captain, I was getting to that part,' smiled the cocky pilot, 'What if we equip my Fire-starter with some of the Plasma weapons we salvaged from the station. Speedy is small enough that it could sneak up behind the ship without detection and I could disable it without giving it a chance to get a shot off.'

A look of genuine consideration and hope appeared on Selina's face, Haver appeared to be doing equations in his head, while Hill just looked unimpressed. 'Captain, I hope you aren't seriously considering this, it is suicide, one fighter against a destroyer, it wouldn't stand a chance and we would still be sitting ducks.'

'He's right SC, I like the notion, but I don't see how it can work. Even with the element of surprise and advanced weaponry you wouldn't get more than a couple of shots before they raised shields and attacked you.' admitted the Captain.

'Haver knows the layout of those ships pretty well from his background in the USSF, as they are basically a copy of a popular design. If he could supply me with a target that would cause them instant and devastating damage, then I could make those first shots really count, then I could have the rest of the squadron back me up.' finished the hopeful Pilot.

All eyes turned on Haver, the pressure mounting on the young genius; the moments seemed like hours as everyone could see he was thinking. A look of excitement flashed across his face, 'The ship's central power core, that would be perfect.' he stated very animatedly.

'Care to elaborate, Mr Haver?' Responded the slightly bemused Captain.

'Sorry Captain,' replied the young Lieutenant whilst he got his bearings, 'The central power core is located on the underside of the ship, just past the engines, the armour there is strong but with plasma weapons and no shields you could just break through. If you hit that it would cause an overload throughout the ship and it would kick on to secondary power, which only controls environmental systems, leaving weapons, shields, communications and engines off- line.'

Laverty thought for a moment, then beamed with a huge smile, 'This plan is completely crazy. Let's do it!'

Within thirty minutes the weapons had been unpacked and were being installed onto Speedy. The Captain had also ordered Engineering Chief White to do what she could to prepare the shields and weapons for a full on attack, just in case SC's plan failed or they needed to back him up.

Commander Hill briefed his marines on the task and the objectives as they would form the boarding party to retrieve the engine components. Although they hoped for the element of surprise, no tactic such as this had been used within the ERF before, no human to their knowledge had ever willingly set foot on a Fedirian vessel. With the Space Station they had been assured light security, but an active attack vessel would be completely different as they had no idea of the level of resistance that they could expect. The risk was high, and unfortunately, the chance of success was low.

One hour after the plan was green lighted the Fedirian destroyer was drawing closer to the moon and Havers' hopes of them passing by the Swan completely was increasingly unlikely. Luckily due to some very fast workmanship Speedy was nearly ready to go and SC was briefing his pilots, as they would provide his back up for the mission.

The overall plan itself was simple, the execution however would be somewhat harder;

Stage 1

SC, in his Fire-starter with the modified weapons, clouded in the radiation from the moon, would approach the Destroyer from the rear and attempts to take out the central power core with as many blasts of the plasma weapons as he could in the available time, crippling the ships weapons, engines and shields and allowing the Swan to dock with the destroyer.

Stage 2

Commander Hill leads his team of marines on board the stricken vessel, eliminates any opposition and retrieves parts to repair the Swan's overdrive system. Also to use the opportunity to gain intelligence and technology from the enemy ship.

It seemed like a good plan; unfortunately, they never did get the opportunity to test it.

The enemy destroyer changed its search pattern without warning and headed straight for the moon, obviously working out where the trail of plasma was heading, pushing the leading Fedirian Commander to decide to save time, realising that the ship they were pursuing may be hiding there. Unfortunately, the enemy craft spotted the Swan before the ERF crew had observed that the enemy ship had changed course, a case of too many jobs to do with not enough people to do them. As soon as the Swan was in range the Fedirian vessel opened fire, pounding its hull with plasma.

Red alert flashed all over the Swan as they hurriedly raised shields and began evasive manoeuvres, Parsons detected the shots coming in and had sprung into action like a coiled spring, doing everything possible to avoid the firepower that was whizzing past the hull. Selina was on the command deck within seconds, silently kicking herself for not keeping a better eye on the approaching ship. Putting her annoyance aside, she began instructing the crew to new actions, trying whatever possible to avoid further damage. They put on as much speed as possible in an attempt to use the Moon as a barrier, circling it so as to not allow the enemy craft a clear shot. Varying their path continuously despite all of this, the enemy ship was still closing in. Surprisingly though, thought Selina, the enemy craft had yet to launch fighters, which was allowing the Swan to concentrate on avoiding one ship rather than several.

In the launch bay SC and the rest of his pilots were awaiting permission for launch; unfortunately, this wasn't possible for him as the engineering crew were finalising the modifications to his fighter and the others were unable to take off as it is impossible to launch whilst the Swan's shields were up. Meaning that in order to launch the support craft the Swan would have to drop its shields, making it even more vulnerable to enemy fire.

'Launch bay! Status report,' the comm system bellowed with the Captains voice.

'Five minutes, Captain, and the modifications will be complete.' replied one of the hanger bay engineers.

'Five minutes! This fight is gonna be over in two minutes, I need the Fire-starters in the air now!' Demanded the Captain.

Two minutes later Speedy was ready to go with SC in place along with his other pilots. The Captain informed them that they would have a short window to launch as soon as the word was given. All Fire-starters were fired up and ready to go; they knew the sooner they departed the sooner the shields would be re-raised.

With Parsons at the helm the Swan slowed down and pulled a tight vertical turn, only possible due to the tightness of the ship's design, allowing them to loop over and position themselves behind the enemy ship. During the back end of this manoeuvre the ship's shields dropped and the seven Fire-starters launched in quick succession from the rear of the small destroyer. Taking the opportunity of suddenly being in an effective attacking position, the Swan opened fire on the enemy ship; however, unlike ERF vessels, the

Fedirian destroyers boast formidable rear facing weaponry, meaning that the Swan had to quickly abandon its position and put the fight in the hands of the Fire-starters.

'Haver, what's the chances of me breaking through that central core armour with the shields in place?' SC asked through his comm system.

'Highly unlikely Commander, that area is too well protected with the shields up.' explained the young Lieutenant.

That news confirmed the Flight Leaders suspicion. He grimaced as he knew they only had a small window in order to defeat this ship, and that window was closing fast. 'Find me another target then! One that will do some substantial damage without blowing up the ship.' demanded SC.

Haver had already pulled out the plans he held of that style of ship and was ferociously studying them for a new weakness. Suddenly, something caught his eye, it bothered him a little that it hadn't been noticed before, 'You could go after their life support, strangely from what I can see that system is not as well protected as the rest of the ship: the armour is weaker there and its lowly shielded.' answered Haver frantically.

The pilot considered the comments, 'OK, sounds good,' replied SC, 'direct me too it.'

Looking back towards his plans, the Operations Officer marked the page for easy identification and replied, 'Topside just past the control section, the hatch should be coloured yellow for ease of maintenance. Good luck, Commander.'

SC maneuvered his craft with Ward formed up on one wing and Karran on the other in a covering formation. Whyte, Santora, Whiterod and Smeaton were providing a distraction for the destroyer's guns. Unfortunately, the only type of distraction available was letting them shoot at the smaller craft. This tactic allowed the strike team to approach undetected. The lack of enemy fighters simplified the manoeuvre as there was only plasma fire coming from the destroyer. SC, along with his escort, approached the destroyer from the rear, keeping their position low to avoid detection, and travelled the length of the enemy ship whilst it had its work cut out trying to lock in on the other four fighters. SC located the area Haver had highlighted, 'Right where he said it would be,' he thought to himself. With a coordinated effort he opened fire along with his escort on the life support systems. The three Fire Starters concentrated their fire and after a few long bursts they broke through the light shielding, landing damage on the armoured hull. Within seconds they had broken through and destroyed the system, witnessing an explosion from within the compartment. It was safe to say the advanced Plasma weapons Speedy was now sporting made all the difference, making it into a formidable little craft.

SC and his fighter escort immediately drew fire from the destroyer and had to take evasive manoeuvres to avoid being hit. Taking his new found firepower, SC located the enemy ships shield array and hammered it with a few volleys of plasma fire, causing mild damage. He then instructed his pilot's to back off to a safe distance and regroup with the Swan. As he suspected, the enemy vessel failed to follow them, meaning at least for now that the Flight Commander's new plan appeared to be working.

From a safe distance Selina and the rest of her crew watched the attack unfold and witnessed the successful damage of one of their enemies' key systems. Selina reached for her comm device, 'Come in SC, are you there?'

'Reading you loud and clear, Captain,' the Flight Commander knowing full well that the remaining officers on the ship would want to know what he had in mind now that the original plan had been blown.

'You did well,' praised the Captain,' they seem to have stopped pursuing us for the moment. So what now Commander? How does this change our previous plan?'

Without pause SC responded, 'Captain, this should make the process easier: a little known fact about Fedirian ships that I picked up back on the moon is that they do not have secondary life support systems, meaning that in about an hour most of the crew will be dead or dying, unless somehow they manage to repair it.'

'So, in theory, we can just walk on board in environmental suits and take what we need to patch up the engines. Very clever.' Selina replied nodding her head and smiling. 'What's to stop them from leaving and going for repair?'

'They cannot go into overdrive with their shields up, and the damage I caused to the array is causing a fluctuation where the shields are coming on and off spasmodically. So they shouldn't be able to get their engines online without first fixing the shields and they don't have the time.' SC replied with an element of smugness, 'In fact if they remain in their current state then we can take their entire ship.'

For the next two hours the crew of the Swan kept a close eye on the disabled ship. At one point it seemed as though they may have fixed the shields, but they started fluctuating the second they attempted to boot up the overdrive, then all of a sudden activity just stopped. Knowing full well that in order to repair the life support system the compartment would have to be accessed from the outside of the ship, it was becoming apparent that whatever oxygen the Fedirian's used must be in short supply.

The Scanners detected no movement aboard the enemy ship, no life signs were showing, the ship seemed adrift, floating without consequence. No attempt had been made to repair the life support from the outside that they could see. The bridge of the Swan was eerily quiet as no one was entirely sure what to do. Had SC been right, were they all now dead and the ship ready for the taking? Nobody knew for certain, but they needed to find out.

'Commander Hill,' bellowed Laverty, the ships second in command arrived by her side on the command deck immediately, 'Prepare your assault team to go aboard.'

The gruff Soldier saluted and responded, 'Yes Captain!' It was evident that the ex-army sergeant was actually looking forward to this raid. From having little control over their situation just hours before, they had now bested an enemy vessel and were about to claim her for their own.

'I would like you to take SC and Haver with you,' Selina insisted. This came like a blow to Hills head; he tolerated SC as he was ranking third in command of the vessel, but the two of them rarely saw eye to eye. Also, Haver was clever, but he was no soldier, and this felt as though it was an extra burden on to his command.

'Are you sure that's necessary, Captain?' replied the ageing military officer, 'My team needs to secure the area before we let any extra people on board.'

The Captain looked sternly at her first officer, 'Yes I am sure it is necessary. Firstly, you need Haver because he knows what you are looking for and where you are likely to find it, he is also better versed in the enemies' systems than anyone on your team. Secondly, if you take the ship and we can recover it completely then you will need a pilot and who better than SC, plus who knows, he might be useful.'

'Yes Captain!' Hill was reluctantly forced to agree. His men were fine soldiers, but knowledge of enemy vessels and how they operate was a little beyond them. He wasn't keen on having outsiders on his team, but if they could be useful then it would be worth having them.

With a few short blasts from the Swan's weapons the enemy destroyer's shields went offline, allowing the ERF ship to come alongside and dock with the crippled vessel. The airlock took little work to open, no explosives required, just a little tinkering by the engineering staff. This was handy as ideally they preferred to take the enemy ship in one piece and not risk any further damage. Hill was first through the hatch and proceeded along the corridor at good pace with his team backing him up, followed closely by Haver and SC, all wearing environmental suits and all armed with hand pistols and rifles, prepared for the possible unsafe and unfriendly environment ahead. Haver was most concerned about this as he had been a computer engineer in his past life, and although he was stationed with the USSF on the Moon, he was never involved with combat. SC, on the other hand, had received basic combat training in the

Navy, but was more of a tactician as a result of his current role as Flight Commander on the Swan.

For the second time in two days Hill was surprised not to have a welcoming committee as he arrived on board, and although it was mostly expected he was no less wary, looking carefully and continuously. The corridor appeared empty, no plasma fire, no shouting, no footsteps, no people, nothing at all, meaning at least for now it was safe to continue. Although, as previously, he thought this was the second time this week that he had boarded an enemy ship without immediate confrontation. However, he also barely escaped the last one alive. Being more cautious this time he requested that Haver check out the computer as soon as possible to ensure that there was no self-destruct mechanism in place this time.

Hill and his team continued through the ship along metal clanking corridors, with dirty metalwork running the length of the ship and flashing light beacons every ten feet, so far they made their way without hazard, clearing rooms as they passed, ensuring the enemy wasn't awaiting them in the dark or lurking in hatches, ready to attack. The current turn of events had everyone on edge, but so far no attack had occurred, no shots fired and not one body found, which everyone was finding a little odd. Despite the eerie nature of this lack of resistance and the likelihood that there may be a trap of some sorts, they still deemed it prudent to split up, with SC leading a team to the control deck and Hill with a second team escorting Haver to the engine room, allowing them to quickly ascertain whether or not the ship was salvageable and whether or not it had the parts they required to fix the Swan.

SC and his team quickly and carefully made their way through the ship heading for the control deck, the plan Haver had supplied them with making navigating around the alien ship relatively easy. The eerie calm and quietness of the journey did little to settle their nerves, as each member of the team expected to be attacked at any moment. Usually people experience fear through waiting or the unknown; however here it was both, they knew something had to happen and they were waiting for it, but they had no idea what it would be. By the end of the journey, SC and his team had arrived and the attack had not come, and there they were standing on the command deck without incident.

First impression of the command and control room was that it was similar in style to that of their own ship, some design differences but a fundamental consistency in the layout, leading SC to wonder if this type of ship had been the inspiration for the USSF ship design, which stood to reason as the ex US Space Force had a bad habit of taking things that didn't belong to them. The irony of the situation was not lost on him that that was exactly what they were aiming to do. SC and his team went straight to work on deciphering the ships systems and getting a handle on how they worked. SC turned his attention to the ships internal sensors to see if he could detect where the crew of the ship may be residing, or more accurately he thought, hiding.

Hill and his team, on the other hand, weren't having quite as straight forward a time as SC. Unfortunately, the engineering bound team wandered straight into what appeared to be an ambush just outside of the engine room; from nowhere an array of plasma fire rained down on the invading party, with no escape possible due to a blast door that had closed behind them sealing the team in. From ahead of them automatic blaster fire was pinning the ERF party to the bulkheads of the ship, leaving the frightened soldiers unable to move It had been pure luck and quick reactions that no one had been hurt, the shooting, although fierce, seemed rather imprecise and allowed the quick moving, fast thinking team to take cover before any real damage was done.

Hill, along with his soldiers, were returning fire but to no avail, as they were shooting blind. There was steam down the corridor blocking their view; as a result they couldn't see any of their attackers. Their return blaster fire didn't appear to be hitting anything as the attacker's firepower was unrelenting. 'We need to get out of here!' announced Haver, who was panicking: this was as far from his comfort zone as he could be.

'If you have any suggestions as to how we accomplish that I would be grateful to hear them!' bellowed Hill, who was becoming less than enamoured with the current situation and was annoyed at himself for allowing a trap to be sprung around him..

'Can we get SC to bring his team around the other side of the engine room and take them out from behind?' Suggested Haver.

Hill rolled his eyes again. He liked suggestions and ideas, but he hated grasping at straws. 'Firstly, we don't know if there is another way in. Secondly, if there is we don't know if that is guarded in the same way and thirdly, the radio is dead, there must be a jamming field up in here, so I couldn't reach SC if I wanted too. I tried that just after the blast door went down.'

The intensity of the firepower failed to diminish and Hill and his team were beginning to wonder if this might be the end. 'I can't let this stalemate continue, I need to try something. I am going to try to and crawl along the floor and try to get a better look at the enemy. Maybe get a better idea of what we are dealing with.' announced Hill.

'That's suicide!' shouted Haver, ' One hit and you're done for.'

'Well we need to do something and sitting here isn't it, I've been watching, the floor doesn't get hit very often.' responded the Commander, having studied the pattern of the blasts he could tell they were sporadic: there was no real aiming involved, just wildfire designed to kill anyone unlucky enough to be in the way, but he suspected there may well be a reason for that.

As Hill prepared to do the unthinkable and Haver was silently praying for a miracle, the Commander began to move along the ground out of cover, slowly unveiling himself to the unrelenting blaster fire reigning down on him and his team. A shot hit the floor just inches from his arm, causing the old army officer to recoil. He suspected he might not reach his target. Just then Haver's miracle had arrived and all enemy fire halted.

A stunned silence made its way through the entire team, everyone afraid to move into the open in case it was a trick. There was an uneasy feeling all around the group, the words of two day before ringing in everyone's head: 'At least if they are shooting at you, you know where you stand.' Even Hill scurried back behind cover, unsure of what the quiet had in store for them. A crackling came through the radio breaking the silence and SC's voice was heard, 'Is everyone ok?'

Hill breathed a sigh of relief and for the moment all the faces in the team relaxed. The Commander replied that they were unhurt but a little confused as to what had transpired. SC explained that he had discovered their plight when he was searching through the internal sensors and that they had tripped an automated defence system designed to trap invaders and eliminate them. Meaning that it had been a range of wall mounted guns that had been firing at them indiscriminately, which had been what Hill had suspected when he had saw the lack of precision in the shots fired. SC had managed to shut off the weapons as quickly as he was able to determine how the system worked. He was grateful that he had been in time to ensure nobody had been hurt.

With access progress could again be made taking very little time for Haver to be able to locate the appropriate parts to allow the chief to repair the Swan's overdrive system. Meanwhile SC, along with some technical help, was able to resume the challenge of repairing the enemy craft back to a usable state. The similarities of internal design was helping their ability to understand how the craft worked. It was during this that SC made another exciting discovery: all navigation, operations, flight and weapon controls had been routed through the command chair, allowing whoever sat in the chair to control all primary functions of the ship, fundamentally making the ship a very big one person fighter,

After discussion with Selina it was decided that the enemy craft was too much of an asset to be left behind, and SC was authorised to bring the ship back to the fleet with the assistance of a skeleton crew. After all parts had been transferred and repairs made to the Swan's engines, along with the new vessel's shields and life support, they would bring the two ships back in convoy. The repairs to both ships had taken roughly four hours to complete and although there was a fear that they may be on borrowed time, the benefits of standing still to make repairs outweighed the risks, as they would soon be able to go to overdrive and would be back among the fleet in a few hours.

'How long until we are ready to depart?' Selina asked the chief engineer and SC through her comm unit.

'The overdrive unit will be up and ready in 10 minutes, Captain.' replied the chief, 'So we can make way then.'

'Enterprise ready at your command, Captain.' replied SC smugly. He had decided to name the enemy vessel after a popular space craft from Earth Science Fiction.

'We will have to speak about that name when we get back to the fleet, I'm sure the Admiral will have some thoughts.' laughed Laverty.

After a short wait the chief announced the Swan was now ready to proceed, both ships making preparations to engage overdrive when alarms started beeping and the sensors flashed up in red.

'Enemy contacts incoming, Captain!' shouted Parsons.

Selina stood up tensed and asked, 'How many?'

'Four,' he replied, 'all the same type as the Enterprise.'

'How far out?' She exclaimed.

'We will be in range of their weapons in 3 minutes.' Replied the helmsman.

Selina tapped her comm unit, 'SC are you seeing this?'

'Yes Captain, I suggest you get the Swan out of here right away, we will join you when we can.' replied SC.

Selina looked confused, 'you said you were ready to go, what's going on?'

'They tracked us too quickly; no way that's a coincidence. I have to assume there is a tracker active on this ship and I can't risk leading the Feds back to the fleet, so we will attempt to hold them off until we can find and disable the tracker.' replied SC.

Ignoring SC's request entirely Selina had Parsons manoeuvre the Swan into an attack position as they prepared to greet the incoming enemy fleet. Realising that his Captain had no intention of leaving him, and knowing arguing the point would be futile, SC manoeuvred his craft into position alongside the Swan, raising shields and arming weapons.

The Swan launched all six remaining Fire Starters, with Ward in command of the fighter group. Meanwhile, the technicians aboard the Enterprise were frantically searching through ship systems, trying to uncover the location of the tracker or anything that could be acting as a beacon.

'Enemy craft in range in 30 seconds!' announced Parsons.

'All hands, this is it, do a good job!' commanded Laverty.

As soon as they entered weapons range the enemy ships opened fire, targeting the Swan initially. This was short lived as the enemy craft that were attacking in a diamond formation suddenly found themselves consumed by weapons fire from the ERF ships that had, with the assistance of the Fire Starters, surrounded the attacking vessels. Instead of her usual craft Ward was piloting Speedy with its upgraded weaponry, which was providing a pounding to the Fedirian ships. Rather than forming a conventional circle, the ERF tactic was to have the 2 large craft constantly circling the enemy, whilst the Fire-starters weaved back and forward throughout the attacking ships. It was an unconventional tactic that was designed to protect the Swan as much as possible. The downside was that this constant movement didn't allow the ERF ships to get any powerful shots on consistent targets. However, it allowed them to buy time by not allowing clear shots at them whilst the crew of the Enterprise searched for the tracker.

'Commander, I think I have found it!' exclaimed crewman Lindsell.

'Good job, can you disable it?' SC responded relieved.

Lindsell nodded his head, 'I think so, I just need to cha...aargh!'

Suddenly Selina noticed that the Enterprise had dropped out of the attack pattern and was now providing an easy target for the attacking ships. She realised that something had obviously gone horribly wrong. The Captain barked new orders, 'All ships defend the Enterprise!' ordered Laverty through the comm unit. Turning her attention back to the stricken ship she pounded her comm unit, 'SC, what's going on?'

The response was silence.

SC had looked up to see Lindsell absorb a Blaster shot a close range. Before he could get a chance to comprehend what had happened he heard another shot fired. SC jumped from the Command chair just in time to avoid the shot. Scrambling back to his feet he grabbed his sidearm and returned fire at the intruder. The bullet hit the enemy in the shoulder. A quick head movement resulted in SC narrowly avoiding another plasma bolt. He took his opportunity and launched himself at the enemy.

The two of them were embroiled in a tussle. The large brown-skinned form had his hand around the young pilot's throat, obviously understanding the effect that this would have on the human intruder. Having reacted in an instant it wasn't until this moment, as SC struggled to survive, that the human actually took the time to look at his alien aggressor. It's safe to say that despite these beings having been responsible for the death of nearly the entire human race, SC wasn't actually sure if any other human being had ever laid eyes on one before. For the most part the Fedirian soldier was humanoid, taller than the average human, possibly around seven foot tall, which was a large part of the reason he had the upper hand on the five foot ten inch tall SC. He was dressed in a dirty grey looking overall, which from the brief touch SC had had it seemed to be similar to an Earth-based poly-blend. The Fedirian had large hands with claw like fingers. The nails were piercing the skin around the human pilot's neck as he throttled him. For a second SC stared right into his enemies face. He could see the brown skin leading up to yellow eyes with black pupils, no obvious ears from the angle he was looking and teeth that looked as sharp as a crocodile. In fact the likeness to a reptile was quite apparent, with a mouth that protruded out from the face. In effect it was like fighting a humanoid dinosaur. The time for observations was over if SC was to survive this. He had to act drastically. Fumbling around, looking for his weapon, caused the larger aggressor to panic and reached to remove the firearm from his opponent. This gave the pilot the distraction he needed and managed to jam his elbow into the Fedirian's face, causing the larger being to become disoriented. SC was able to get more movement from his arms, which he used to grab the weapon and let out a couple of shots and finish off his attacker. The pressure he had experienced on his throat made it hard for him to find his voice to call for help, but it was unneeded as the shots fired led engineers Williams and Michaels to come running in. They looked confused by the situation, but went straight to helping their Commander remove the large seven foot body off of him. SC returned to the command chair as quickly as he could. 'Michaels, get that thing out of here and make sure it's dead! Williams, Lindsell found the tracker, he was working there, take a look, hopefully you can see what he was doing?'

Williams hurried over to the control panel directly next to Lindsell's body and quickly ascertained what it was he had found. He took no time getting to work and within a minute he had dis-engaged the tracker. 'That should do it Commander, tracker is disabled.'

'Selina!' shouted SC as he tapped his comm unit, 'It's time to go!'

With the instruction to depart given, all Fire Starters returned to the Swan in double quick time, performing back to back emergency landings. Both ships quickly engaged their overdrives and made a run for it out of the system. Leaving behind a wake of destruction and disappointed enemies, the Fedirian craft would attempt to follow, but after 3 or 4 course changes it would become impossible for them to track the fleeing ships.

Chapter 4

The three static ships which comprised the majority of the ERF fleet made a sight for sore eyes as the Swan and the Enterprise arrived. Despite having successfully returned from the mission, with a new ship in tow, there was nothing quite like the security of being within a large fleet. Only the O'Neil was missing from the full complement of ERF Vessels; however, this was to be expected as the whole fleet was never usually altogether. Travelling in convoy had been the usual situation for the ERF, who found comfort in having the safety of numbers. However, the threat of attack and annihilation meant that it made more sense to have at least one ship missing at all times, leaving someone else to take up the fight if the fleet were to be lost. Until the arrival of the Enterprise, the fleet hadn't reduced or expanded in number since their escape from the Moon base one year before. With the carrier known as the Dreadnought, the destroyer Valiant' and the frigate Alexandra normally travelling together, and with the O'Neil and 'Swan' normally sent on scouting, research or tactical runs, the addition of the powerful tactical frigate Enterprise caused a great deal of excitement among all members of the fleet.

Both the Swan and the Enterprise docked on either side of the Dreadnought, allowing the swift transfer of engineering teams and parts between the vessels as they worked frantically to make both damaged ships one hundred percent operational again. Being such a small fleet meant that they couldn't afford to have any ships out of commission for any length of time.

The Swan would require extensive work due to the condition of the hull; the fireball that had engulfed it hadn't missed a bit of paintwork. Repairs such as this would take longer and were more difficult due to the lack of a dry dock where the work would be easier, with the ability to access the outside of the ship more readily. The Enterprise, however, had relatively minor damage and would require far less time to repair, though it was drawing a crowd for a different reason entirely. This was the closest that anyone in the ERF had gotten to a Fedirian ship since the war began, and now they had one of their own. This was the best opportunity that the ERF would get to examine the technology and ship designs for weaknesses that could lead to an advantage.

Admiral Vocke marched through the hatch and took his first steps on to a Fedirian space craft, with the look of a conquering General. Caesar himself would have been put to shame with the entrance; however, this was a day of celebration. After witnessing the devastation that this ship and others like it had caused, he took it to be a serious victory for him and his fleet to now possess one. A former Captain of a German Naval Vessel he quickly took command of the ERF after the evacuation to the moon base. Never having married or procreated, he was unencumbered by thoughts of personal loss after the attack, although the effect of losing one's home and planet was more than anyone could just ignore, especially for a military person, who enrols to protect and defend. However, without personal grief and with his background, he seemed like the obvious choice for leadership. This would allow him to concentrate on the main goal which was survival, rather than what everyone else wanted straight away, which was revenge.

Inspecting the Enterprise alongside Vocke was Vice Admiral Lewis, SC's former commanding officer from the HMS Edinburgh, a fair and likeable man. The attack on Earth left him broken after leaving behind a wife and daughter, not knowing their fate and being powerless to search for them. Initially Lewis took command on the moon base, but he quickly realised that his personal feelings wouldn't allow him to impartially lead the fleet without attempting to settle his own scores, so he happily relinquished command to Vocke and took the role of Vice Admiral, making him second in command of the human race.

Heading straight for the command and control room, Vocke and Lewis passed a number of engineers who were studying the ship's systems from remote terminals; they walked through the grey corridors and escalated the two levels to the command floor. On entering it became instantly apparent to the two high ranked officers how alike this ships control room was to that of the ERF ships. It didn't take a genius to realise that their lineage was probably the same, meaning there was another race out there somewhere with this design that both humans and Fedirians had stolen.

Through the bustle of engineers now filling the control room Vocke noticed Captain Laverty standing with Lt Commander Cave. Standing for a moment he continued to take in the rest of the scene around him before heading to the ships' captors with Lewis following closely behind. The two lower ranked officers moved to attention and saluted the Admiral and Vice Admiral.

'Captain, I look forward to your report. I saw the Swan on my way here, it looks like quite a mess.' stated the Admiral bluntly, 'In fact, it's good that you returned with another vessel, otherwise if there was to be an attack the fleets safety may have been put at a further risk.'

As hard as it was the Captain of the Swan remembered to bite her tongue. 'I assure you sir the damage to my ship could not have been avoided.' replied Selina, with only a slight trace of hostility in her voice, which was hard as she was struggling with the fact that his mission could have killed her and the entire crew.

'We will see, I will determine that after studying your report.' replied the Admiral smugly.

Though annoyed, Selina responded in the only way her training allowed, 'Yes, Sir!'

During this exchange SC stood glaring at the Admiral. He was not as skilled at diplomacy and locking his emotions away as his Captain. The aggression on the pilots face had apparently not gone unnoticed by the Vice Admiral, who was returning a glare at SC in an attempt to warn him off of any stupid action that he might be considering.

Unfortunately, the Vice-Admiral's attempts at peacekeeping were too little, too late, as it only took the slightest glance in SC's direction for it to be noticed by the Admiral.

'Something on your mind Commander?' asked the Admiral sharply.

'I was just wondering when the thank you, well done and I'm sorry for your loss were coming?' Replied the Lt Commander, with very obvious sharpness and hostility in his voice.

The Admiral looked at SC incredulously, 'Excuse me Commander?'

The look from Vocke told SC everything that he needed to know, that the Admiral wasn't willing to take any responsibility for what happened or show any gratitude for what had been achieved. Self-control disappeared from the Fire Starter pilot, causing him to lose his temper. 'Well let's forget the apology to Captain Laverty and the rest of the crew for intentionally sending us all on a suicide mission by failing to inform us that the space station was set on a timed self-destruct, resulting in the loss of a vast number of our crew. If it hadn't been for the actions of another brave Captain then we would have all been dead. Putting all of that aside and concentrating on the only thing you actually care about, which are material possessions, so at the very least I would have expected would be that you would have thanked our Captain for not only retrieving what you sent us for despite the circumstances, but also for the added bonus of capturing an enemy ship in a usable condition for the fleet. We obviously don't expect you to show any remorse or understanding for the loss of a lot of good people!'

'Commander, these issues are none of your concern. Your job is to follow orders, but I must inform you that your rudeness will not be tolerated. I am your superior officer and you have no right to address me in this manner. If you continue in this vain you will find yourself confined to the brig.' responded an irate Vocke.

'You say "superior", I say merely higher ranking.' shot back SC. All thoughts of respect and position were gone now. A glance towards Selina showed a dumbstruck look on her face while she struggled to comprehend how to respond to the outburst by her third in command.

'That's enough Commander, you are out of line.' interjected the Vice-Admiral.

'No it's ok, I can handle this John,' replied the Admiral to his second in command. Controlling his tone carefully, he turned back toward the young officer, 'Tell me, Cave, just why should I thank you and your crew for doing your job? In case you haven't noticed this is the Military and as I am sure you are aware it is of course your job to follow orders. Or did you think this rank system was just an honorary thing? We are an armed military force and that's what we do here.'

'In case you have forgotten we are also all that is left of the human race, to ensure survival of our race we cannot afford the luxury to blindly follow orders, especially as you expect us to die for you or your poorly thought out schemes!' fired back a steamed up SC.

The Admiral maintained a smug look on his face and continued to bait SC with another flippant comment, 'You are still alive, aren't you? So I would say that the plan worked perfectly, my "scheme", as you put it, achieved the goal. Again, I fail to see your issue.'

The expression on SC's face was one of rage, despite the warning prods from his Captain. The young officer was not about to back down to the smugness of the older man, 'Over a fifth of our crew are dead as a result of your plan and your orders, the only reason the rest are still here is down to resourcefulness and a bit of luck, combined with the arrival of the O'Neil, which literally saved us from complete destruction. You may see us all as expendable, but when there are so few of us left then every life counts.'

The Admiral had lost the look of smugness and was beaming with arrogance and irritation, 'We are in a war, you little shit, and every single person is expendable in a war! I will continue to throw as many bodies at this enemy as I need to in order to win. When people die in conflict it means simply that the weaker ones are being weeded out to help the stronger survive!'

What happened next wasn't planned or thought out, but simply a reaction based on intense emotion. It was like the whole event took place in slow motion. SC swung his fist hard, catching the Admiral square on the jaw, causing him to hit the ground like a ton of bricks. After what felt like a minute had passed, though in reality it was a few seconds, nobody moved, they all just observed the Admiral lying like a crumpled mess on the floor. As soon as he regained his senses the Vice-Admiral grabbed SC by the arms and held him, instantly calling for security officers to take the Lt Commander into custody. The pilot turned to look at his Captain, who was open mouthed in disbelief.

Selina dropped to the floor to check on the Admiral who was coming around after the shock of the sudden attack. The silence was deafening as no one spoke. Two security officers arrived and held SC, who was putting up no struggle at all. It was the enraged Admiral who broke the silence, 'You're finished Commander,' rubbing his bruised and tender jaw, 'I'll have you marooned on an uninhabited moon for this. Take him to the brig!'

SC was quickly escorted to the brig, so quickly in fact that he couldn't even remember the journey, not sure his feet even touched the ground. Needless to say this was not his finest moment; however, he couldn't help but feel completely justified in his actions and found it impossible to regret what had happened. Before he knew what was going on he was locked up in a small cell, no larger than eight feet by six, with a small, single bed attached to the wall and a combined toilet and sink unit. Although used to sparse accommodations on board the Swan, this was a stage further, an even smaller and less comfortable metal box. SC hoped that this would not be for long, although he did start to worry about what would be next.

As it turned out SC's hope for a speedy resolution to this situation was not to be granted, as a week later he was still confined to his cell. A separate, special punishment he very much enjoyed, isolated with the exception of the guard bringing his meals. He was allowed no visitors, in the week he had been incarcerated he was yet to see a friendly face. After the first day of not seeing anyone, SC had suspected that visitation had been prohibited; as it had now been a week, he knew it to be a fact. Although he never suspected that he was the most popular guy on the ship, he still would have expected to have had at least one of his pilots coming to check on him. Despite the boredom, the silence was great for clarity, even if it was driving him a little stir crazy. Left with only his thoughts for company, he was imagining all the worst things that could be about to happen to him. What was going on outside, how were the ships and the people? He also spent a lot of time thinking about the past, what had happened since the Moon escape and reflecting on what had been done and achieved in this time.

SC's thoughts went back to the day of the moon attack; It was heady thought to think his whole family and the majority of people he knew were now dead, his home gone, destroyed by invaders from another world, all in the blink of an eye, nothing would ever be the same again. SC, like many others, had felt so much bitterness towards the situation, losing almost everything in his world due to a situation that he had no knowledge of, something which perhaps could have been avoided with careful forethought. Although he knew that there were always decisions made without public knowledge, this one had proved to be a grave mistake.

SC was aware that he was one of the lucky ones: not only was he still alive, but due to his last few years in the military, he hadn't lost everyone in his life, there were people that he knew that were still alive and were working beside him to try and survive.

Two people in particular he was glad to still have with him were Selina and Naomi, both who had become close friends of his due to him serving beside them on the Edinburgh. Naomi had been the chief deck hand and trainee helicopter pilot that he saw every day, especially as she was directly responsible ensuring that his helicopter was tied down and maintained when it was aboard ship. They often chatted about family and friends back home, as it turned out that they grew up a few miles from each other and knew a lot of the same people. It was nice having someone from home around, even though they had never met before. Having someone who was from the same place was even more important now, especially with how likely it was now that anyone else they knew from back then was more than likely dead.

Selina was SC's direct superior on board the Edinburgh and had been since he was stationed there. Although they shared none of the history that he had with Naomi, the two of them clicked instantly and were completely on the same wavelength, and although he could never admit it, with her being a senior officer, SC had always had a crush on her. Maybe things would be different now there was no real military, just a rag tag group of survivors building ships to take them to safety.

Amazingly, routine was quick to set in and his day had become quite standard by this point. Having been on the moon for 4 months, he slept and he worked, there was no real socialising as the moon base held no real facilities for it, even just staying up late at night was frowned upon, the additional power usage raised the threat of detection from the enemy. So curfews were instated, as if they were all staying away at camp as children. It all became his normal routine, waking at 6am to be showered, he would get dressed, in one of a few altered USSF uniforms, as these were all they had stored in abundance. He would be at breakfast at 6.30am for ration packed eggs and bacon; there had been over one million packets of that particular vacuum packed ration pack found, so it made sense to utilise it for breakfast purposes. There were so many vacuum packed rations and tinned food on the unused space base that it made him suspect that the US government might have expected something to happen, they were so well prepared. He would then travel to the hanger bay where he would carry out training all day, breaking briefly for a short lunch, finishing at 6pm before going for dinner, which would be whatever tins were to be opened and heated that day, then lights out by 8pm. Thinking back, it was a strange existence he had experienced on the Moon, although just at this moment he missed it.

On this morning he remembered walking to the hanger bay for flight simulation training as usual, he linked up with Naomi in the corridor, which happened almost daily, and they chatted their way along the metal covered tube between one of the habitat domes and the metal infrastructure that was housed inside the rock of the Moon. It was then that SC heard an explosion; it was fierce and it was close, the corridor he and Naomi were standing in shaking violently. Once they recovered from the shock of the blast both SC and Naomi bolted down the metal corridor towards the hanger bay. When they reached the hanger it was obvious to see what was happening: the situation they had feared for 4 months, the base was under attack!

Pilots, engineers and deck hands were running about everywhere. Blind panic ensued; this was no well-oiled military machine, this was individuals frightened for their lives, and after the last attack they had faced who could really blame them. SC spotted the Flight Deck Commander and headed straight to him, with Naomi following close behind.

'They found us!' The always unflappable Commander stated. 'We are implementing an emergency evacuation.'

At that point another explosion shook the hanger bay, causing pipes over-head to detach with a small explosion of flash fire. 'What do you need us to do?' requested the pilot.

'We need time, son! We have no idea how many ships are out there or how long this base can hold up; We need time to evacuate.' replied the Commander with the first sign of fear that he had ever shown SC, stress and worry glistening in his eyes.

'Aye Sir! I will grab as many pilots as I can and we will try and keep them busy for a while.' SC replied.

At that moment another explosion shook through the complex and a conduit above their heads exploded. 'Hurry!' shouted the Commander.

The sharp clunking of the door made SC wake up from his day dream: he was back in his cell in the brig and he had a visitor.

'Well aren't you the stupidest guy in the galaxy!' Bellowed Ward.

'Naomi, how lovely to see you. Are you sure there's not something else you should be doing? I mean, I've only been here a week. Why not wait longer next time?' SC replied sarcastically.

'Well as you don't want to see me I'll go then.' Ward turned to leave.

'Get back here!' Scolded SC.

'You know I would have been here earlier if I could have. It was the situation, there were orders.' offered Naomi.

'Against seeing me?' responded SC.

'Yeah, you don't get to punch the admiral of the fleet then just to chill with your peeps. You really stirred up something. There has been monumental arguments about how to deal with you.' Stated Ward.

SC smiled, 'Yeah? Who was on my side?'

Naomi shrugged, 'The Captain of course, but actually the majority of the senior brass support how good you are,.I heard even Hill spoke to Lewis for you.'

'That was probably to put the boot in, he isn't my biggest fan,' laughed the prisoner.

'You know, I don't think it was. To be honest, nobody really wants to see you locked away in here, it's just nobody knows what to do with you. This isn't like old Earth military when you would have been court marshalled out; we are so far away from civilisation. I just know that you're gonna have to come up with something amazing to get out of this.'

SC and Ward chatted on for a little while longer, her bringing him up to date on the status on the fleet. He was thankful of the company, and then all too soon she was gone, leaving him once again alone. Although SC enjoyed having had some company and the update on what was going on, he was no closer to figuring out how he would get himself out of his current predicament. Laying back down on his bed he closed his eyes and drifted slowly off.

He was back at the day of the moon evacuation, this time in the cockpit of his Fire Starter, now known as Speedy. He was finally getting to put the theory and training in the simulators into practice. He, along with twenty more fighters, were engaging a fleet of ten enemy warships: the fighting was intense and lethal, as the warship weapons and armour completely outmatched the ERF Fire Starters. However, the small fighters were capable of far superior manoeuvrability, allowing the small craft to carry out a constant series of hit and run attacks, using a ratio of two to one- as suggested by SC- and they were able to engage all ten enemy ships, drawing their fire away from the weakened Moon Base which was rapidly being evacuated. The plan was working well and the fighters, though inflicting little damage, were so far avoiding being hit. The pilots knew that they didn't need to destroy these enemy ships: SC had told his team to just give them something else to shoot at. However, after a little time, one of the enemy ships got wise to the diversion tactic and shrugging off its small attackers and made a beeline for a large transport ship that had just begun to make a run from the moon. Unfortunately the two fighters were powerless to stop it, failing to even slow the enemy, as with little warning the warship bore down on the transport and pounded it with its blasters. This transport ship was still being constructed when the attack had begun, and the engineers hadn't yet outfitted it with energy shields. They tried to run but the enemy craft was too fast and within minutes the ship was destroyed in a fiery explosion, eliminating any chance of survivors.

The destroyed transport ship had just over one thousand people on board, who had scrambled to it as if it were a lifeboat; now they were dead, causing the next single greatest loss of human life since the day of the initial attack. Committed to a path of destruction, the enemy warship set its guns on a new target, the fleet's largest ship, the carrier. Although a large, intimidating ship, the weapon systems are underwhelming, as it exists to carry large amounts of people and equipment and was not intended to be in the thick of the conflict. So it was to be the next victim of the Fedirians. As the warship closed in on the carrier it opened fire, looking to cause carnage, but behind the enemy craft appeared the Destroyer known as the Swan, 'Open fire, all weapons!' came the order from the ship's Captain, Selina Laverty. The Swan's undetected approach had given them a significant tactical advantage over the enemy ship and with the assistance of two Fire Starters, they obliterated the warship.

With all ships now clear of the moon and at a safe distance to engage overdrive engines, the fighters turned and fled from the enemy ships, heading straight for the Carrier and the Swan. The pilots staged emergency landings into the hangers of both ships; with all fighters back on board, the Swan and the Carrier took off into overdrive headed for the rendezvous.

It was at that rendezvous the ships divided up crew and fighter support, and the tally of losses were calculated. Around 1500 dead or missing in total, there were around 1000 to 1100 on board the transport ship, and there had been fatalities in the hanger prior to launch, some elsewhere in the base due to explosions and fires. All 1500 had been counted as dead due to the hurried nature of the evacuation; not every person could be accounted for. SC started to think about the bodies that must have been left behind, four hundred people dead on the moon. Four hundred bodies just lying around, where? Although the base was a sizeable facility it was never built to house six thousand people: they lived in close quarters, four hundred people making up a significant portion of the remaining human population. Yet nobody mentioned stepping over corridors filled with bodies, which surely there would have been if there had been so many dead. So it stands to reason that they just didn't make it on to the ships, but how, the Carrier took off forty five minutes after the start of the attack, the entire base could be crossed in under 15 minutes at a walking pace and he couldn't imagine anyone wasn't running that day. The habitat spheres generally housed 500 - 800 people, was it possible one of the spheres had been cut off? If so, what happened to the people? Did the Fedirian's destroy the base and them with it, or is it possible they were still there?

Chapter 5

SC spent the majority of that night going through thoughts in his head about the Moon facility and the possibility of anyone still being alive there. The confident officer was also giving a great deal of thought to every encounter they had had with the Fedirians over the past year. His thought train was suddenly disturbed with the clanging open of the brig door.

Standing in front of him was a flushed, out of breath Ward. It was apparent that she had run to see him in a great hurry, which had exhausted this very athletic fighter pilot. 'What's wrong?' He asked sharply, seeing the urgency in her face.

'It's Riley,' she replied, 'he is in critical condition, the O'Neil is back and she is wasted. I'm surprised she is still flying, what with the state she is in.'

'How many casualties?' SC wanted to know.

'Not sure, no one has had a chance to do a count, but it looks like the Command Centre took the worst of the damage. Hopefully it may be lighter than what we had.'

SC thought for a moment, then spoke, 'Find out what you can, then get back to me.'

'Will do,' replied Ward, before turning and disappearing back out the door, leaving her Flight Commander sitting alone in the cell, feeling completely useless, unable to check on his old friend and wanting payback for whoever hurt him and his ship.

Ward ran along the metal corridors of the Dreadnought, the loud banging of her steps resounding all around her and right down the shaft style walkways. Eventually she reached the docking port where the O'Neil was anchored. Wounded personnel were still being removed and engineers were trying to cram themselves through the small space to get on board the ship as medical teams struggled to remove the injured. She couldn't help thinking that we didn't need an enemy; we were quite capable of working against ourselves. It was then she saw the reason for the disorganisation: the Admiral was standing barking orders at Maguire-the Chief of the O'Neil's engineering staff- demanding that he get the ship operational again as soon as possible. Commander Jamieson, Riley's second in command, was standing pleading with the Admiral and Maguire to give him some time to evacuate the wounded and the bodies before the engineers started ripping the ship apart. The Admiral insisted that security of the fleet depended upon having functional ships and as Riley and Laverty had seen fit to cause significant damage to theirs, the fleet was no longer secure.

Ward couldn't help but understand why SC had decked him, although she knew the Admiral wasn't completely wrong: the fleet was far from secure, as the Swan was still out of commission, with the engines having to be completely rebuilt. It looked as though it would be a further week before it was fully operational, although she understood most of the structural work and weapons had been repaired. This just meant that if a conflict was upon them, they could stand and fight, they just couldn't run anywhere.

Seeing that the O'Neil had come back with her Command Centre blown out completely, it seemed that it was destined to be docked for some time. However, Ward wasn't sure how much difference a couple of hours would make to this situation and felt that they should be able to clear the ship before starting repairs. She had also found out that the new addition to the fleet, the Enterprise (name set to be changed by the Admiral), was out of commission also. In trying to figure out how they had tied all the systems together they managed to cut out all functionality, so the engineering staff were already in trouble from the Admiral over that situation. Deciding to lend a hand, Naomi helped the medical staff clear some people through the docking hatch, and played traffic warden for a little while, letting medical teams leave and getting the engineering gangs on board in a more organised manner. After a while it started to sort itself out and nobody was able to give her any new information, Ward went off in search of Haver, as he usually knew something.

Without needing to look for long she found him working on the Swan, sorting out the tactical systems, which he now told her were fully operational. But as she had suspected, he confirmed that the ships engines would be down for at least another week. He had tried to get on to the team to work on the Enterprise, but the Admiral had stated that no one from the Swan would be allowed to go near the ship, citing as his reason as they had enough work to do fixing their own ship. However, they suspected that SC's conduct had led him to believe they were all in some way disloyal and couldn't be trusted. Haver, like Riley, had been part of the USSC and had more knowledge of the enemy ships than any of them, especially as he had met and worked with the species who they stole the designs from in his position as a ship builder on the Moon. Understandably, he was feeling particularly pissed off at the exclusion. It became obvious that Haver had been working in a bubble and that he didn't have any new information on what had happened to the O'Neil, or on the condition of Captain Riley.

Eager to get some new information, Ward wandered down to the medical bay. Outside the operating theatre where Riley was being worked on was Commander Jamieson, who had evidently came down to stand vigil for his Captain after having had no luck negotiating with the Admiral. Away from everything and near his friend was a good place to cool off as it was evident that he was still agitated. Taking advantage of the fact it was just the two of them present Naomi started quizzing the Commander, and although Ward didn't know Jamieson particularly well, they had met before. Without much nudging he started to tell her what had happened.

The O'Neil had arrived in the Zora sector as planned; they were told that there was a disused mining colony on one of the moons, so they were there to check it out and see if it could be used as a temporary home for the fleet. Unfortunately there was nothing there; they had found remains of a structure, but it had been totally destroyed, there were no walls standing. They decided to carry out an overall sweep of the sector to find out if there was anything of interest, but after a day of searching all they had found was empty rocks and no planets suitable for humans.

Just as they were about to head back to the fleet they detected the signal of another ship nearby. It didn't appear to be Fedirian in origin, so the decision was made to check it out. In the year since they had been out there they had not encountered another species other that the Feds, so this was too good an opportunity to pass up.

As they approached the stricken vessel, Riley recognised it as a USSC ship, the Eagle. It was one of the Older ships that they had, but it was big: when first built it would have held a crew of two thousand and was roughly the same size as the Dreadnought, the ERF's carrier, but much better armed with twenty rotational blaster cannons, ten missile launch tubes each carrying a payload of two hundred nuclear warheads. Riley hadn't realised it had survived the battle of Earth, but here it was, sitting right out in the middle of space, making no movements whatsoever.

Riley knew this to be very suspicious and attempted to make contact with the ship. When no answer came he knew something was definitely wrong, ordering the ship on to full alert. He was prepared to strike at a moment's notice. The O'Neil took up a position alongside the ship as if preparing to dock, knowing that they would have to drop shields if they were to complete the manoeuvre. Sensing a trap, Riley had his operations chief rotate the shield harmonics to create the illusion that the shields were being dropped, when really all they were doing was changing to a different frequency. As soon as the rotation was started an explosion erupted from the docking point on the Eagle. It was an outward explosion, causing minimal damage to the USSC craft, but would have engulfed half of the O'Neil had the shields been down. Luckily all it did was put a dent in the shield power and gave them all a good shake.

It was at this point three Fedirian vessels appeared from behind the moon in attack formation, heading straight for the O'Neil. Expecting to be facing a heavily damaged, vulnerable ship the enemy were surprised when a fully functional O'Neil came towards them, all guns blazing, targeting the weapons systems on the first ship, using evasive manoeuvring to avoid as much plasma fire as they could from the other two ships. The concentrated fire broke through the shields and took out the weapons on the first ship; quickly changing direction, they targeted the second ship coming round behind them, showing immense skill and tactics. Unfortunately, the third ship was still hammering the O'Neil from the side. Although trying to avoid the assault, they did not want to give up the position behind the second ship, otherwise they would have heavy firepower from two ships rather than one to deal with.

Taking advantage of the position behind the second ship, the O'Neil concentrated their fire on its engines. Although taking a beating themselves, they hung out long enough to cripple the second ship's propulsion. Reducing the enemy fleet to one ship evened the odds of the conflict; however, the O'Neil had lost shields and was taking damage, this time without the ability to gain position on the third ship. They were the mouse being chased by a much stronger cat. Riley needed to turn this around, as he knew they stood no chance of outrunning the other ship. So, he ordered all crew aside from himself and the helmsman off of the command deck as the tactic he was about to use would expose the bridge more than any other place on the ship. Taking control of weapon systems himself, Riley told the helmsman to invert the ship, exposing the underside so it was now facing upwards. As soon as this movement was completed the O'Neil pulled hard, up which is a full speed vertical turn which would bring them up on the underside of the enemy ship.

The biggest problem with this manoeuvre is that during the turn the Command Centre would be unprotected and exposed to enemy fire. Considering the O'Neil had no shields left, this would be especially dangerous. However, the weak spot on the enemy ship was the underside; if they could concentrate enough firepower long enough on one specific point, they could break through the shield at that point and take out the central power core, leaving the enemy ship dead in space. Normally it would take an excessive amount of firepower to break through-certainly more than they had time for- but the O'Neil was carrying one nuclear torpedo, which if they fired that at just the right moment would cause serious damage.

As the O'Neil was pulling up on its turn the enemy ship redirected their fire power towards the command deck, doing exactly what Riley had thought- but hoped- they wouldn't do. Steadily, the Captain encouraged the helmsman to hold his course as the hull was taking the damage for the moment and had yet to breach; he just needed an extra twenty seconds to get into position. The enemy firepower came harder and harder, eventually causing a hull breach. The command Centre of the O'Neill was shaking violently and systems were exploding all over. It was all Riley and the helmsman could do to stay at their consoles. The hull held out just long enough to let the O'Neil get into position. Locking on to target, Riley fired full weapons at the concentrated spot on the enemy craft. The advantage with the new firing position was that the enemy ship could no longer get a good lock on the O'Neil, allowing them to pound away at the Fedirian ship. Drawing ever closer to the enemy, Riley left it to the last possible point to launch the torpedo. Maintaining gun fire on the enemy ship, he had the helmsman pull away just before the torpedo impacted the hull. Success was theirs, with the nuke hitting its mark, and it caused severe damage to the enemy vessel.

Unfortunately, the O'Neil pulled away too late and the explosion shockwave from the torpedo impacted the critically damaged Command Centre of the O'Neil. The damage was extreme, blowing a large hole straight through the hull. Riley and the helmsman would have been sucked straight into space if it had not been for the emergency force fields, which activate automatically on breach of the hull. However, both Riley and his helmsman were in critical condition as the explosion and breach caused mayhem around them and they suffered burns and bruising from falling equipment and exploding consoles.

Jamieson quickly took command of the situation, rerouting basic helm control to the engineering deck and ordering the crewman nearest to get them out of there. He monitored the condition of the enemy ships from his console; that's when he realised the ship they had just nuked was behaving very strangely. He could detect multiple internal explosions and before he knew it the third ship had completely exploded, the damage caused had obviously set off a chain reaction on board resulting in complete destruction.

As soon as the O'Neil began making tracks he ordered medical teams to retrieve Riley and the Helmsman from the Command Centre. He also ordered the Engineering chief to carry out a damage assessment, starting with the command Centre and then throughout the rest of the ship.

The overdrive function of the ship could only be activated from the helm unit in the Command Centre. Due to the damage inflicted to that part of the ship the overdrive was not able to function; this meant it took the O'Neil days to get back to the fleet. Although the Captain and Helmsman were still alive, their condition was critical.

After leaving a still distraught Jamieson, Ward returned to see her Flight Commander and relayed the story in its entirety.

'Any news on Paul?' SC asked.

'Not yet, they aren't saying anything other than he is stable but still critical.' replied Ward.

'Did Jamieson say what happened to the USSF ship?'

'Nope, I guess that means it's still with the Feds.' speculated Ward.

Ward left SC to some quiet contemplation. He thought some more about the situations that had been happening of late; combined with the O'Neil's encounter, finally he reached a conclusion. He called for the guard outside his cell with urgency in his voice and demanded, 'I need to see the Admiral, Now!'

Having not come to any conclusion as to what to do with SC, the Admiral had been happy to lock him away and forget about him for the moment. So when he received a summons from the unpopular prisoner he wasn't inclined to go see him; however, Vice Admiral Lewis convinced him that it may be worth going to speak to him, for all his faults he was still a good officer. Although the Admiral disagreed with the premise he did agree to visit the brig. He was not willing to let SC out to discuss anything, but he would speak to him through bars.

The atmosphere of the meeting was frosty to say the least, but true to his word, the Admiral came to listen. Vice Admiral Lewis was also in attendance with the intention of keeping the peace. Once all parties were there SC started explain his theory. Starting with the notion that there may still be people alive on the Moon, he conceded that it was speculation, but he made the point that there was sufficient reason to assume that it could be true. Although Lewis agreed there was some merit to the argument he failed to see what had changed to make SC think that there was anything they could do about the situation.

This led SC on to his next point: how many Fedirian ships were still functional within the area? Assuming the initial attack on Earth was the full complement of ships in the area, and they had no real reason to doubt this, they attacked with forty ships, eight of them were destroyed on the day of the initial attack and one was destroyed during the escape from the moon. The Swan and O'Neil destroyed another two at the space station last week and captured another one, two days later. The O'Neil destroyed one and crippled two just a few days ago. That initial number of forty had reduced to twenty seven ships, maximum. Those twenty seven ships seemed to be spread out in groups of twos and threes throughout this region of space. Within the last couple of weeks they had been picking away at them.

The Admiral put forward that they had no idea whether or not the Feds had had reinforcements within the year, so there was no way of knowing the size of force the ERF were up against. SC countered the senior officer's argument by reminding him the Enterprise had been captured due to there being only one enemy crew member aboard; it stood to reason as the controls had been configured to be flown by one person, SC had taken that to mean that if there had been reinforcements then they would have diluted the crews to refill the vessels that were lacking. The USSF had been in space for a long time before the Fedirian's attacked Earth, isn't it reasonable to assume that it may take a few years for new ships to turn up? So this could be our best chance to take back Earth's solar system, they have six ships and when at full strength we have the ability to succeed at a ratio of one versus two, with fighter assistance. One year ago there only were nine enemy ships left in orbit of Earth; it might be possible that that fleet has been watered down as well.

'One more ship.' stated the Admiral.

'Excuse me Sir, what do you mean?' Responded Lewis.

'We would need one more ship before I would consider this. I wouldn't want the Carrier in the thick of the fighting, we have too many people aboard, and it is my opinion that the carrier may only be used for support from a distance. Five versus nine aren't good odds, six versus nine are much better. We need another ship.'

Everything went quiet for a minute with all eyes on SC. Suddenly it came to him. 'You want the Eagle,' stated the young officer as it became clear what the Admiral was suggesting.

'Yes!'

'You want me to get it for you.' SC's brain started to kick in, figuring out a way to make it happen.

'Yes!'

Vice Admiral Lewis, looking on with disbelief, exclaimed, 'That's suicide, there is no way for one person to sneak into an enemy controlled area, get aboard a ship whose condition is questionable, with who knows how many enemy combatants, disable two enemy ships and bring the ship back in one piece. Plus the USSF ships can't be piloted by one person. It's not possible!'

'Except it might just be,' replied SC with a dry grin on his face, 'it just might be.'

Preparations were set in motion to ready SC for the mission; although, it wasn't to happen quite the way Vice Admiral Lewis had suggested. SC would not be sneaking past the enemy ships: he would be going in all guns blazing. The plan SC set out would be for him piloting Speedy to be dropped off just outside the system where the Eagle was located. They would have to use the Enterprise to drop him off as the Swan's engines weren't back online yet. That meant the Admiral was forced to let Haver on board the Enterprise in order to fix it. Working on the understanding that the enemy ships were possibly still under repair, owing to the reduced manpower in the enemy fleet, Speedy with its advanced weaponry would be able get close to the targets and quickly disable them. Then using a remote docking bay transmitter provided by Haver, SC could open the fighter bay doors on the friendly ship and land inside. Once secure he would call in the Enterprise,' which would be carrying extra personnel and would allow the Eagle to be brought back into the fleet.

As was to be expected, Selina Laverty was not happy about the plan at all and insisted that they should wait a few days and then the Swan and Enterprise would be battle ready and they could make it a decisive victory, or at the very least if they didn't want to wait, she thought they could back SC up with the stolen Fedirian vessel. The Admiral argued that they couldn't afford to lose the time, if the ship moved they might not find it again, and as the Enterprise wasn't battle ready he could not afford to risk it to go in and support SC.

SC knew this was likely a suicide mission, but it was his only chance to be active within the fleet again, and if he was successful then he could pave the way home for the ERF, which that meant more to him than anything. He also knew that if he could destroy the two guard ships then the Fedirian Fleet would be weaker still. This was also a win-win for the Admiral; if SC failed he had gotten rid of a pain in the arse without having to kill him himself, but if he succeeded then he would have been responsible for bringing home another powerful ship for the fleet.

Haver was allowed to accompany the mission as it was likely that he would be required on board the Eagle if SC got it cleared. Jamieson was given temporary command of the Enterprise for the mission, as he was the only person with command experience without a working ship currently. Speedy docked with the Enterprise (name still to be changed shortly by the Admiral), and the strike team was ready to go. The mission included around twenty people overall, keeping the risk ratio to a minimum amount of potential losses, with the biggest potential loss being the Enterprise in the Admirals mind.

The Enterprise took off at full overdrive, expecting to be at location in roughly three hours. Leaving behind a hopeful fleet and a determined Selina, who was hard at work with all the engineering teams to fix the engines on the 'Swan'. She knew it was likely that this mission could go south quickly, and they may need back up, so she was out to make sure that she was in a position to help, no matter what the Admiral had requested.

Four hours later the Enterprise arrived just outside the system. They proceeded to carry out long range scans; the results were inconclusive, meaning it was unclear if any of the ships were still in the area.

'Unfortunately we are too far out to give you any useful intelligence, Commander.' stated Jamieson.

'I understand Sir,' replied SC.

'You know we can't help you if you get into trouble, I have strict instructions to turn around and head back if we lose your signal for any reason,' stated the Acting Captain.

'I appreciate the lift, Captain. I know what I signed up for.' nodded the eager pilot.

The acting Captain nodded back, 'Good luck Lt Commander. Let us know as soon as you have anything to report.'

With that SC launched Speedy and headed into the enemy controlled system. Keeping his sensors at the setting for their furthest point, he was constantly on the lookout for the first sign of enemy vessels. SC didn't have to wait long: flashing up on his long range sensors was what he took to be the Eagle . At least that confirms that they are still here, he thought to himself. As Speedy was passing by a small moon the pilot detected a strange signal, not a ship as it was too small, in fact too small to be any kind of structure, but the signal was there. Deciding to check it out before heading in he guided his Fire Starter towards the source of the signal. It soon became apparent that it was being emitted from the surface of the moon. On closer inspection SC could see it was a ship tagger, similar to a trip wire: it detected ships entering the system and no doubt relayed the message back to the enemy ships, allowing them to setup their surprise attack. It was such a subtle signal that Speedy only detected it because the craft was so small it doesn't create the same wash as a cruiser or destroyer like the O'Neil.

Adjusting his course, SC manoeuvred around the moon in such a way that Speedy wouldn't be painted with the signal, allowing him to sneak in on the enemy without detection.

Once he cleared the moon, SC hopped from planet to moon, using his proximity to them to mask his approach. Within about twenty minutes he came around a moon and could see the Eagle, with two enemy ships nearby, both ships looking the worse for wear, sporting a good degree of damage. SC could tell that neither ship had their shields raised, taking it that this was due to them believing they were alone and not falling into the belief that their shield systems weren't working.

Luckily due to how the trap had been set up to lure in the O'Neil, the hostile vessels were positioned close to a moon, which is where no doubt these ships would have been hiding. This meant SC could use the same trap against them; however providing their shields were actually working, it would likely take them seconds to raise, meaning he would have to make the first shots count. He was very aware that by the time the pilot would complete the attack run on the first ship the second one would be on him. So SC would have to identify the strongest ship and try to disable it first, leaving him to play cat and mouse with the second, weaker one. He couldn't perform an internal scan of the ship's systems without risking detection, so he would have to base his decision on what he could see. The ship closest to him had some scoring on the bottom of the ship where the central power core was, meaning it should be vulnerable to attack. The other ship didn't; with the exception of a lot of scoring to the engines, it was looking rather healthy. Typical situation, SC thought to himself, the closest ship is the weakest one, meaning he would need to fly past it to take out the stronger ship. Realising there was no safe way to do that without being detected, SC had to make the decision to do exactly what he didn't want to do, disable the weaker ship, leaving the stronger one to attack him.

Chapter 6

SC adopted the safest approach vector that he could, guiding Speedy as close to the enemy ships as was possible without being detected. With weapons charged to full power he took his run at the closest ship, carefully targeting the enemy's central power core. He unleashed the full power of his advanced weaponry upon the target. The scoring on the hull was obviously worse than how it looked because the armoured plating gave in much quicker than expected, causing SC's attack to produce exactly the result he was after: destroying the central power core completely on the short run. However, an after effect that he hoped for but couldn't have counted on also took place: the destruction of the power core caused a ripple effect throughout the ship, creating multiple mini explosions, resulting in the enemy vessel exploding completely. Luckily for SC he had already beat a hasty retreat back towards the moon, from where he had emerged, narrowly escaping the blast radius of the ship. The other Fedirian ship wasn't so lucky. Despite being able to raise shields in time, the explosion seriously weakened the protective fields, reducing them to thirty percent of available power. The attack had completely disorientated the remaining ship, having raised the shields when they detected their counterpart about to detonate, they hadn't had a chance to scan for the ship that had attacked them. Now there were no other ships aside from the Eagle registering on the scans. However, a quick scan of the debris from the explosion revealed that it was consistent with only the destroyed vessel and no other ships, immediately looking to the obvious source of the attack- but it was obvious that the Eagle hadn't moved and the Fedirian commander detected no trace that the former USSF ship could have fired.

The Fedirian Commander realised quickly that the attacking ship must still be out there, as evidently the attacker had not been destroyed in the blast. A quick search showed that there were no new contacts registering on the scanners. The only obvious hiding place for a ship capable of destroying their comrade was the Moon: the enemy must be using that for cover. With fully charged weapons he directed the ship toward the Moon, preparing to hunt and destroy whatever he found. Slowly the Cruiser circled the grey Moon, the pilot's eyes trained to the screen and not the sensors: he was a hunter, looking for prey, he didn't need the technology, and he would follow his instincts, as his people had done long ago. Although he did not know what his opponent looked like, he knew it must be a powerful beast to have destroyed his partner so easily, so there was no way that they could hide for long. Slowly and sharply he made progress 'round the small planet sized obstacle, concentrating hard on any move or shape that his eyes detected. Either his eyes were deceiving him, or there was nothing there to see.

Unfortunately this throwback to his hunting ways was to be short lived, as his instincts betrayed him and, despite what logic dictated, it was as though there was nothing there, meaning then that the Fedirian Commander must be being stalked by his enemy. It was now that his technology had a place, turning to his scanners for confirmation. He could still detect no other craft around, which was impossible, how could this powerful ship move so stealthily around this Moon and so quickly that it didn't declare itself on the scanners, and was not visible to the eye? The whole situation didn't make sense. He needed to find it, his prey- he needed retribution. Turning back to his screen he studied the display for any signs of movement; nothing was apparent. He became distracted quickly by the sound of alarms that started beeping, and by the effect of the ship shaking mildly. He looked to his scanners for explanation but nothing was apparent. how could there be nothing there? His shields were now registering at twenty seven percent. How could he have been attacked and there be nothing there? Alarms started ringing again and again through the large ship, followed by the same shaking that had happened before, shields now registered at twenty four percent and still nothing on the scanners. To be so accurate with these shots the ship would have to be able to see him, but then why couldn't he see them?

SC was enjoying being so small in this situation. He was travelling below the Fedirian ship, but keeping so close to the moon that his signal was completely masked, allowing him to drop back a little and carry out a quick attack run on the enemy without showing his position. As good as this was he knew he wouldn't be able to carry it on for much longer, as the enemy would soon realise where the attack was coming from, and if Speedy was to be hit by one good shot he would be dead. This meant time for more decisive action. As good as it was to keep taking three percent of the shields here and there SC knew he needed to make more of an impact before he was discovered. Figuring one more attack would cause the enemy ship to change his tactic, SC setup for a big attack run. this one would expose him, so he knew that it would need to count.

Emerging from the moon, weapons trained on the central power core, SC unleashed his full weapons power on the enemy vessel. It didn't take long for the highly focused Fedirian Commander to detect the weapons fire, the pilot immediately attempting to take evasive action. Unluckily for the defending craft, the attempt was unsuccessful as the attacking vessel was so small. This did however, allow the first opportunity for the Fedirian to see his attacker. He was astounded to see how small it was, especially for how much punch it delivered. Insulted at being stalked by such an insignificant craft, he wanted badly to destroy it, so he opened fire in the direction of Speedy. Fortunately the Fedirian vessels inability to evade the small craft meant that SC had been successful in taking down the enemy vessel's shields. He had, however, now lost his attacking angle on the central power core, and the turn of events had him head to head with the much larger vessel. Playing chicken was not SC's idea of a good strategy, but it did seem to be the only one he was left with. Doing his best to avoid the attacking firepower, he was dodging and weaving closer to the enemy craft; he became unable to escape the field of fire, so although not getting hit, he couldn't escape the tirade of plasma fire surrounding him. The predicament put an end to any chance of cat and mouse games or targeting weak spots; all he could do was continue on this course toward his enemy and try not to get hit. It looked unlikely

SC would survive this encounter, so all that was important was that he take the enemy with him. Targeting all fire power and setting Speedy's course on the ship's Command Centre, he pushed forward at full power. The speed of the approaching fighter made it impossible for the Fedirian to get a weapon lock on the smaller craft. The larger destroyer was firing everything he had, directly in front of his ship; suddenly explosions started occurring all around him, the command Centre was falling apart and he could do nothing about it. SC quickly realised he was getting through the armour and stepped up his efforts, resulting in the enemy firepower stopping. SC realised the ship was about to explode, pulling up just as the ship was engulfed in a massive blast, with the wave catching the escaping Speedy before it could get clear.

'Captain!' Helmsman Harris aboard the Enterprise was fixated on his Screen looking puzzled.

'Yes, Harris.' replied Jamieson.

Still staring at his Screen, the Helmsman spoke slowly, 'We have lost the signal coming from SC's Fire Starter.'.

'Are you sure?' inquired the Captain with a look of dismay.

'Yes Sir, it's no longer transmitting.' Replied Harris.

'Set a course for the fleet, we better report back immediately.' ordered the Captain.

Haver turned to look at the new Captain with a pained expression. 'Pardon me Sir, but shouldn't we wait a little bit longer, or go and take a look perhaps?'

Jamieson turned to look at Haver 'Our orders state we leave now, we can't risk being detected. Make it so, Harris.'

The Enterprise turned around and fled from the area, heading back to the fleet at full speed. This mission they all thought was a long shot, was now in complete failure.

After a few short hours they arrived back at the fleet, the Enterprise docking with the Dreadnought. Jamieson had barely disembarked when he encountered Selina. 'What happened?' Demanded the Swan's Captain, knowing full well that they had returned far too quickly for the mission to have been successful.

'It's over, I'm sorry but he's dead, the mission failed.' responded the new Captain matter-of-factly. Selina looked like she had been shot through the heart. Falling back against the bulkhead, she just stood stunned with her mouth open and her eyes welling.

Jamieson walked on. He could see the Admiral waiting for him. Haver approached Selina and put his hand on her shoulder and said, 'I don't think he's dead, Captain.' Selina looked to him with confused eyes.

Haver didn't waste any time filling in his Captain on what had happened. Selina looked shocked, then rage entered her eyes. With Haver in tow she marched over to Jamieson, Lewis and the Admiral. 'You just left him there!' She shouted.

Jamieson was startled by the sudden accusation. He started to mumble, 'I had no choice, I was following my orders.'

'How could you!' Exclaimed Laverty, looking as though she may punch the much taller Officer.

'Calm down Captain!' Ordered Lewis, 'he was ordered not to follow without an all clear. Without a tangible signal he needed to abort, we couldn't risk the Enterprise being discovered.'

'So the life of one of our best people means nothing to you!' She exclaimed.

'He knew the risks, in-fact it was his plan.' responded the Admiral with a smirk.

'Well you might be okay to leave him, but I'm not.' Laverty replied.

'What are you saying, Captain?' Responded Lewis.

Selina turned around and walked away, looking over her shoulder she said 'I'm going back for him.'

'No you're not, Captain! Come back here!' shouted the Admiral, all traces of smugness gone.

Selina kept on walking with Haver close behind. Ignoring the shouting officers at her back, she turned to her Operations officer and said, 'We better move quickly.'

It was cold in the cabin as SC woke. For a minute he wondered where he was; his head was aching, he could feel that there was blood trickling down his face. He investigated with his hand, although it was stinging. It seemed as though it was only a surface wound. Everything started to flood back to him. It was obvious now that he had survived the explosion, he was still alive. It took another minute to shake off his dizziness, and then he started checking his systems. How long had he been out? he wondered, looking at his instruments. It seemed as though it hadn't been more than about thirty minutes. Speedy was in a bad way; he knew the ship was drifting, but all this time in hostile space he knew he was lucky not to have been picked up. The small craft had minimum propulsion, no weapons functioning, life support was running on minimal- actually it seemed that the system was failing. SC thought the air was seeming a little thin, and that certainly explained the loss in temperature. Scanners weren't functioning at all so he couldn't tell if there was anyone left to fight with, not that he could of if there was. The radio had died, meaning he was unable to call for help. Without many options available to him the young pilot set a course for the Eagle, which just seemed to be drifting aimlessly in space. No movement since he had arrived, no visible attempt had been made to move, run or attack. Not knowing what the situation was on-board did not fill the pilot with confidence, but he knew he had no choice other than to go in blind and try to figure it out.

Using the hanger bay door opener that Haver had provided for him, he slowly entered the launch bay, finding what seemed like a safe place to land. He was amazed to see that there were about a dozen Fire Starters like Speedy still sitting parked in the Hanger. They looked launch ready, just without any pilots. He exited his craft slowly, taking his sidearm with him as he went, knowing it was likely that he wasn't out of trouble yet, and headed for the exit hatch. It was like walking around a ghost ship. SC was getting a little tired of this spooky feeling; every enemy craft or station lately had been deserted and eerily quiet, but there was

always another shoe to drop. The young officer just wanted
to make sure it didn't drop on him. Using standard protocol
he made his way to where he understood the Command
Centre to be. He needed to find a working radio so he
could get in touch with the Enterprise, if it was still there.

Encountering no resistance at all SC reached the Command
Centre quickly. On inspection all systems apart from life
support had been powered down. Unlike the Fedirian ship
all the systems on this vessel hadn't been tied in to one
control point; it seemed as though you would need at least
five people to fly this ship due to the spread of systems
over the consoles. Being unable to spread himself five ways,
SC became even more aware of the need to find the radio
as he was going to need some help. After a little searching
he located the communications system; however, like all the
other systems, it was powered off and it wasn't immediately
clear how to get it back online. It was obvious he would not
get help anytime soon, so he needed to make sure of his
surroundings. Internal Scanners weren't operational, so no
chance of searching for other life signs. SC turned back to
the one system which was working, life support. Every area
was set to normal running level throughout the ship, which
was quite low due to the absence of crew, with the
exception of the cargo bay which seemed to have a higher
than normal draw. In fact it was quite a bit higher, as
normally these barely register for life support and now
seventy percent of the whole ships usage was there. It
became apparent that there were definitely other people
aboard; it's just right now he had no way of knowing if they
were friend or foe.

He knew he needed to investigate, but the aching in his
head and dizziness from his ordeal were making him feel

sluggish and he badly just wanted to sit and rest for a while. But the environment wasn't exactly safe, so he had to move. SC took his time heading towards where the ship's way finder told him the cargo bay was. Not wanting to disturb any unfriendly characters on board the ship, he would have to try and determine the occupants of the room before he entered, providing they weren't waiting for him already. He approached the corridor containing the entrance to the cargo bay. Walking softly he stopped at the T-junction connecting his corridor with that one. Taking his time he looked from one side to the other but could not see any people standing guard, nor in fact could he see anyone at all. Deciding to continue on to the door, SC did his best to remain silent as he walked along the metal corridor. He arrived at the door with still nobody else in sight. There appeared to be an external lock on the door, meaning it had been locked from the outside. Presupposing that whoever was inside had been locked in there, that still didn't provide any guarantee of the occupants being friendly. Not wanting to assume anything, as he was well aware of the Fedirian's enjoyment of setting traps, SC put his ear to the door to see if he could hear anything from inside.

Unfortunately due to the thickness of the metal, the room was well soundproofed and SC was unable to hear anything at all. Although it was possible to disengage the lock from the outside, SC was nervous about suddenly unlocking the door to release whatever could be waiting inside. Stuck with few options, he proceeded to access a maintenance tube that was located next to the cargo bay, giving him an opportunity to try and see or hear what was going on in the room before risking opening the door.

SC climbed the ladder within the maintenance tube. This would take him up four decks, over the top of the cargo bay. It was cramped and the air inside the tubes was very thin, making SC very tired and a little weak. Normally portable ventilators were worn inside the tubes due to the lack of air vents within. Not wanting to waste the time searching for one, SC elected to go without; however, now just getting to the top of the cargo area and feeling very faint, combined with his ongoing dizziness, he was regretting the decision almost immediately. Reaching the top of the cargo area he carefully looked for an access point so he could observe the situation within the room and get some air. He didn't need to crawl along very far before he reached the first hatch. Slowly he opened the access panel, taking care to be completely silent. He took his first look and, more importantly, his first breath of air. The sudden influx of air made him a bit dizzy and he nearly fell into the hole created by the hatch door being open.

The weary pilot caught himself and surveyed the sight in front of him. What he saw was enough to make him lose his breath for an entirely different reason. Human people, hundreds of human people. Just sitting and standing around, talking. Their clothes looked a bit tatty but no more than you would expect of prisoners, or in fact people without the opportunity to update their attire. They seemed normal, just imprisoned within this large room, and he could get them out. SC quickly made his way back along the tube and down the ladder, barely catching his breath when he got to the access panel at the bottom. SC worked on opening the lock. It took longer than he thought it would, partly due to giddiness caused by oxygen deprivation, and the other part caused by the excitement of finding more people alive. Once the lock had been disabled, SC paused for a second before opening the hatch, unsure what sort of welcome he would receive. He knew he needed to be composed. Slowly SC opened the hatch, taking his time so not to frighten anyone inside. As soon as the door was fully open he was met by confused and surprised faces, then suddenly a man shouting 'Wait! Stop!' and SC hit the ground with a thud.

SC opened his eyes, but the light made him close them again. He was feeling a little sick and the lights seemed bright; slowly he was able to open them properly, and the blurriness started to wear off. For the second time in about two hours he was coming round from unconsciousness. His head wasn't thanking him for it. As his eyes cleared he saw a group of people, a large group. He then heard a woman voice shouting, 'He's waking up!'

Very soon he had a crowd surrounding him; the pilot became very aware he was still lying on the ground. His head was propped up but he was definitely starting to feel quite vulnerable, so he tried sitting up, to almost instantly fall back down again. His body was still a little dizzy so he decided to remain in the propped up position he found himself back in. Actually, this is comfortable, he thought to himself. Through the crowd emerged a large domineering man, dressed in a blue uniform; from what SC could remember it looked a lot like the uniform Riley had been wearing when he first met him. A number of people around him seemed to be dressed similarly, so it stood to reason, taking into account the ship he was on, that these were USSF crew members.

'Sorry my friend, I thought you were something else, so I had to give you a whack.' stated the large crew member.

'No worries, I'd have done the same myself. How long was I out?' Asked a groggy SC.

'Only a few minutes. I'm glad you have come round so quickly; I was beginning to worry about you, plus we are eager for an update on what's going on. How many of you are there? Where are the Feds?' Asked the same crew member. 'Oh, I'm Derek, by the way.'

'Nice to meet you Derek, I'm SC. Ok so where do I start.'

SC quickly explained that he was on his own. He was assuming his back-up had left as they hadn't had any contact from him. He let them know that he had destroyed the surrounding vessels and was here to recover the ship for his fleet, taking care not to give away any other details about the size or location of the fleet, just in case. These were humans, but they weren't ERF, so he wasn't entirely sure how much information to trust them with.

Derek briefly explained that the remaining USSF ships had split into 2 separate forces due to a difference of opinion on how to proceed after the fall of Earth; one half of the fleet wanted to search for a new home the other half wanted vengeance against their attackers. Derek and the crew of the Eagle were part of the fleet supposed to be hunting the Fedirian's; they were on an information gathering exercise when they were ambushed by four ships. They destroyed one, but the other three knocked out their engines and weapons. They were ordered by the Fedirian's through the intercom to get into the cargo bay; if they didn't the ship would be destroyed. Reluctantly they agreed with the demand. Within an hour of them closing themselves in to the cargo bay they heard something outside and when they went to check it out they realised that the door had been locked from the outside. The crew was trapped, and although they could have possibly escaped if they wanted too, they didn't know what the situation was outside the door.

'Why didn't they just cut life support to the cargo bay and suffocate you all?' SC asked.

'They couldn't,' answered a wiry looking man, ' I locked out the computer so they couldn't use it.'

'This is Cliff, Head of Operations,' replied Derek.

'Ok, that makes sense,' replied SC, 'Oh, by the way, how many of you are there on board?'

'At last count, 552.' answered Derek.

Pleased at the massive new additions to the numbers left within the human race, SC decided it was time that they got moving. Whilst in a non-functioning vessel they were a sitting duck for attack. The Captain of the Eagle had died during the attack, which had left Derek in charge. Accompanied by Cliff and a few other crew members SC headed back to the Command Centre. The rest of the crew went back to standard stations, with a few more than normal heading to engineering to try and get the engines back online. SC recommended engines over weapons as they needed to get moving just in case the Fedirian ships that they had destroyed weren't working alone.

Cliff rebooted all the systems and the command Centre sprung back to life. SC attempted to contact the Enterprise to see if it was still out there, but with no luck. Assuming that they had headed back to the fleet rather than been destroyed, he knew he didn't have much time, otherwise the entire fleet may have moved by the time they got there. Unsure of where the rest of the USSF fleet were, Derek had agreed to head to the ERF when they got the ship moving.

The report came back from engineering that if they had a day, then the team could have the engines fully back online, but instead they could have the ship moving again in two hours on standard power and try to fix the Overdrive en route. Two hours would have to be good enough; in the mean-time, they also got to work on the weapon systems, as they wouldn't be moving particularly fast, the ship may need some firepower to deal with unexpected visitors.

Before too long the standard engines were online and the ship was moving, trying as hard as possible to put some distance between them and the debris of the enemy vessels. Unfortunately they hadn't been moving very long when a ship was detected on long range Scanners.

'Ship incoming!' Shouted Cliff.

'Let me take a look,' responded SC as he needed to ensure it wasn't one of the ERF vessels. 'No I don't recognise it, it must be hostile. it looks as though the course it is on looks like it's heading to our previous location.'

'How long before they detect us?' Asked Derek.

'Any minute, I would think,' replied Cliff.

'Status of weapons?' Demanded Derek.

'Minimal power to blasters sir.' hastily responded Cliff.

'Hide.' directed SC.

Unsure of the correct action, as this was his first time in Command, Derek took note of SC's suggestion and had the helmsman move the ship close to the moon of a nearby planet, hoping that the proximity would mask them. It was a worrying few minutes for the crew of the Eagle; however, the plan worked and the enemy ship flew past them without detection. As the ship went past they were able to ascertain that it was indeed a Fedirian vessel and they had had a lucky escape. As soon as the enemy was clear of scanner range the Eagle started moving again, aware that the ship could come back at any-time.

The Eagle was making steady progress; at its current rate it would take a few days to get back to the fleet. However, SC was hopeful that if engineering could get the overdrive back on line then they would be only a few hours from safety. This was the second time in two weeks that he had found himself in unknown space on a damaged ship; the pilot was very aware of the dangers. He wanted the ability to run away fast and be only a short distance from armed support. SC wished that Speedy was in better condition, as with its advanced weaponry it was a force to be reckoned with. At the moment, however, it was in need of some serious mechanical attention.

SC was right to be concerned, as within an hour of the first encounter with the passing enemy ship it was back. Cliff was shouting at Derek, the ship was scanning them and catching up fast. They had two minutes until it would be on them. Unfortunately, there were still no shields working and weapons were still at minimum power. 'We are dead!' Exclaimed Derek.

'Get the pilots into the Fire Starters,' commanded SC, 'it's our best chance to keep them off of us.'

'FireStarters are no match for Fedirian Frigates,' responded the new Captain.

'Trust me, we are going to help them, but we need the extra firepower,' replied SC.

Derek gave the order for the pilots to launch and engage the enemy ship. In the meantime SC was working with engineering to boost the weapons power, fully aware that they needed the bigger guns if they were to have any chance of surviving this. The only way to increase power to the weapons at all would be to divert it from engines, which would leave the Eagle as a sitting target. Guns or movement was the choice, and Derek could not make the decision.

The Fire Starters were doing a good job of hit and run on the enemy ship and had slowed it slightly; however, it was now closing into weapons range of the Eagle., The time was here to either turn and fight or try to avoid and run. The lack of speed prevented them from being able to run with any commitment, and the lack of weapons power would make fighting suicide. Everyone in the command Centre was looking to Derek, who looked at SC. 'What do you think?'

'It's your ship, all I have is risky and likely won't work.' answered SC.

'If we don't do something we are gonna die anyway, so I think we will take risky.' replied a resigned Derek.

SC nodded and took charge of the situation. 'Helm, all stop, engineering transfer all power to weapons, tactical prepare to fire at the following target. Squadron Commander concentrate firepower along with the Eagle.'

The Eagle stopped suddenly, so suddenly in fact that the Fedirian ship flew straight past them. However, as the enemy was passing, the Eagle, along with all of the fighter support, opened up fire on the underbelly of the enemy craft, breaking through the enemy's shield, and causing scoring to the underside of the enemy ship. Unfortunately the firepower of the USSF ship wasn't strong enough to break through the armour protecting the central power core in such a short space of time, allowing the Fedirian ship to take itself to a safe distance, whilst rotating their shields to protect their obvious weak spot. Turning into attack position, it set its sights on the static vessel. Derek turned to SC and said, 'it was a good try my new friend. I'm sorry it had to end so soon, but I'd sooner go out fighting than running away.'

'Yes Sir,' replied SC, 'or maybe not.'

'Ship incoming!' Bellowed Cliff.

The Fedirian ship started to take serious damage to its hind quarters. Trying to turn to face its attacker, it took more damage all around. Being back within weapons range, the Eagle- along with the ten Fire Starters- opened fire on the enemy.

'Hit it with everything we've got!' Demanded Selina Laverty.

The force of firepower from all the attacking craft caused the Fedirian vessel to lose shields completely and take on serious damage all over. Within seconds the enemy ship exploded in an array of fireworks. Cheering erupted from all over the Command Centre on both the Eagle and the Swan. Through the communications unit on-board the Swan SC's voice could be heard, 'Selina Laverty I am going to kiss you on the mouth for that most amazing timing.'

The Captain blushed and smiled and was treated to a chorus of wolf whistles and cheering. 'Lt Commander, must I remind you that you are addressing a superior officer.' she joked.

'I would happily do time for that you little beauty.' he replied.

'I'm glad you're ok too.' Selina smiled.

Both ships linked up and Laverty was the first to board, straight into the arms of SC who hugged her tightly whilst raising her off of the ground. He introduced his Captain to Derek and Haver to Cliff, who both quickly went off in search of engineering with the express objective of getting the engines working properly so they could get home. With the Swan standing guard and Haver assisting with the repairs they got the Eagle's overdrive properly operational again in only twelve hours, allowing both vessels to travel back to the fleet side by side like the conquering heroes that they were.

Chapter 7

Old grievances were forgotten for now, with the Admiral welcoming SC and Selina back like heroes returning from war, bringing with them a shiny new powerful ship and another 552 human beings to the fleet. For the first time in months there was a feeling of jubilation amongst the ERF. The sudden realisation that they weren't the only humans still in the galaxy made everyone feel a little bit less endangered.

'Congratulations Commander, your bold plan worked out,' applauded the Admiral.

'We wouldn't have been here if it wasn't for Captain Laverty and the crew of the Swan, sir.' stated SC matter-of-factly.

'Well, quite. Well done Captain,' the Admiral bumbled awkwardly.

SC introduced Derek to the Admiral and began the debrief, the head of the fleet insisting that the new captain bring him up to date on the state of the USSF, including manpower and fleet size. Derek did his best to answer what he could, explaining that ten USSF ships had survived the invasion of earth, and to his knowledge all were still flying. They had had a combined crew count of around six and a half thousand; obviously he had no way of knowing if that number had changed. He could only speak with any real knowledge about his half of the fleet, which had five ships and about three thousand people. Although, as more than five hundred of them were on board his ship, the number in his old fleet had now considerably diminished. When asked about the location of the rest of his fleet, Derek couldn't help: they changed position constantly and, he had been out of touch with them for too long whilst they were imprisoned and didn't have any knowledge of the new rendezvous.

Without much persuasion Derek agreed to bring the Eagle into the ERF as he was grateful for their efforts to rescue them, and he knew better than anyone that it was considerably safer to travel in a convoy than as a single ship alone; however, he may have reconsidered had he known exactly what the Admiral was planning.

Very quickly repairs were underway on all ships, whilst plans were set in motion for the big attack. SC had spoken to Derek previously about the plan to retake the solar system, and he was excited to get involved, liking their odds of a mass attack on the Fedirians and taking back what was theirs. So for the next two days, every ship was checked and fixed; engines, shields, weapons and life support were given priority. Non-essential personnel were moved to the Carrier in order to ensure minimal casualties when the attack would begin. Riley had recovered well from his injuries and would be available to lead the now fully repaired O'Neil into battle. The ship's helmsman, however, was not quite as quick to recover; though still alive, his injuries were more severe, leaving him not in any real condition to resume his post. He would require at least a few weeks of recovery.

A meeting was called on-board the Dreadnought of all senior officers, the Admiral, Vice Admiral Lewis, Captain Hatherly from the Dreadnought, Captain Riley of the O'Neil, Captain Laverty of the Swan, Captain Derek Strong of the Eagle, Acting Captain Jamieson of the Enterprise, Captain Taylor of the Alexandra, Captain Clarke of the Valiant, Commander Sharples of Fleet Medical, Lt Commander SC-head of Fire Starter Operations- and Lt Commander Wilson, head of Fleet Engineering.

A meeting of this type was a very strange event, what with having all senior officers of the fleet in one place normally regarded as being too high a security risk; if anything was to happen to them, then the fleet would be left without any decision makers or trained leaders. But this meeting was an important one, as SC understood it this was the official announcement and planning of the operation to take back Earth.

All the officers were seated around an oval table with the Admiral seated at one of the points. The room settled down and he stood and addressed the awaiting officers: 'We have had a good week; there have been some negative issues and some injuries, and there has been death, but there has also been salvation to the tune of five hundred and fifty two new members of the ERF; we have had two new ships join our ranks. Although not the most powerful, our fleet of seven vessels is formidable: this, along with the knowledge that there are at least another six thousand humans out there in the galaxy, is remarkable news. This news brings us hope, for a new way forward, a real chance that the human species will survive, and a new resolve for the future.'

The entire room applauded the Admiral for these wise words of hope. SC started to wonder if he had been wrong about the Admiral; it seemed that he did care, and although SC didn't like his methods, the job was a very difficult one, and maybe he was leading them forward well. The Admiral continued: ' I hope you will all join me in welcoming Captain Strong to the fleet, we are most glad to have you.' The room erupted into applause again. It was obvious that they hadn't had anything to celebrate in a while as everyone was getting very excited.

'Captain Strong, you couldn't have joined us at a better time. It is time. It is time for decisive action, it is time to stand up and it is time to strike back!' Before the Admiral had even finished the sentence the applause had begun, chorused with cheers. SC laughed at the theatrics of it all, but he couldn't help but get carried along. After all this was his plan about to be announced; feeling proud, he was cheering along with the rest of them.

'As of three days ago we estimated the Fedirian fleet in the area to be around twenty seven ships; the events of that day changed that count to twenty four. However, we now learn from our new friend, Captain Strong, that his division of the USSF were responsible for the destruction of a further four vessels, bringing that count to twenty. Suddenly a war of seven vessels versus twenty doesn't seem quite so un-winnable.' The Admiral rested for a moment, letting the information sink in to all at the table.

'As of this time tomorrow, we start our new campaign: to rid the universe of the cancerous species called the Fedirian's!'

There was a look of slight shock on the faces of every officer at the table, including SC, who was trying to work out whether or not this was the same plan that he had spoken to the Admiral about. Was this just grand standing or was this the actual plan? Captain Clarke was the first to speak. 'What exactly are you suggesting, Admiral?'

'We have received intelligence from the Enterprise computer that there is a medium sized fleet holding position in the Lambda sector, protecting a small space station. We will attack that fleet and take control of the space station. Once we have that station we will harvest all the tech we can before destroying the structure.'

Now it was SC's turn to speak: 'With all due respect, sir, what about Earth? And the people on the Moon?'

'There is no guarantee there is anyone on the Moon,' answered the Admiral. 'As for the Earth, we will get there eventually, once we have destroyed every one of those wretched creatures.'

Selina looked alarmed, ' Admiral, do you mean all the Fedirians in this area, or all of their species?'

'The whole lot of them!' Shouted the Admiral. Everyone was a little shell shocked for the remainder of the meeting. It was true that no-one had any love for the enemy, but what the Admiral was suggesting was genocide, which didn't sit well with a lot of them. However, knowing the Admirals' propensity for flying off the handle, everyone remained quiet, even SC.

The Admiral set out the plan of attack: all seven ships would arrive together, the Dreadnought would hold back, providing assistance with its long range guns and tactical missiles. The remaining six ships would engage the enemy ships on a two-on-one basis. Although there was no accurate intelligence on the size of the fleet at the station, it was believed to be three to four enemy vessels. The station was also armed, so the attacking ships would concentrate on their assigned target, destroy it, then move on to either another enemy vessel or the space station. The Fire Starter support craft would engage any extra enemy vessels and fighters; however, one squadron would remain with the Dreadnought to provide protection in case any ships got past the attacking fleet.

The plan itself was sound and although SC wanted the next target to be Earth, it did make sense to take out a few weaker targets first, thus reducing the overall size of the enemy garrison. However, he wasn't interested in a long campaign of eradication; aside from the time involved and danger to themselves, a merciless attack upon an entire species would make the ERF no better than the Fedirians. For now though it made sense to carry out this raid, as if the intelligence was any good, it would get them one step closer to going home.

SC worked out the fighter detail with Naomi, and although he had planned dozens of attacks, he was used to having only a few Fire Starters in his plan. Now he had fifty, not counting the ten that would be guarding the carrier. Being sensitive to the normal allocations of these craft was essential, as he needed to keep people who were used to working with each together whilst integrating them into a co-operative plan. SC had also been warned by both Ward and Laverty that under no condition should he be taking heroic action. There was to be a large attacking fleet and it made no sense to take on too much himself. In theory that idea was sound, he thought, but in practice it's a different story; plus, he had the best armed small craft in the fleet, more was expected of him. He would plan on no more than to lead the squadron and take charge of his part of the attack.

There was a real sense of tension in the air; although the fleet had not departed yet, everyone was gearing up for battle, a situation that had not happened before. Not voluntarily, anyway. Selina was carrying out last minute system tests on the Swan, preparing for the attack. She needed to know her tough little ship would be ready; the last full scale assault it had been involved in nearly destroyed it and the crew. She was not willing to have that happen again. It made her feel better that the whole fleet would be by her side, and SC, she was glad he would be there, fighting right next to her.

The military created difficult relationships, putting you in harm's way where you have to rely on the people you serve with. There is a closeness that you have with them, a bond that is stronger than friendship. However, you were not allowed to take those feelings any further. Passion, desire, love are all normal progressions of those feelings, but they are forbidden. Things were different now, almost every living person was counted as military now, so maybe it was time to change those rules, as the only way the human race could survive now was for people to be having babies, which is impossible if fraternisation is forbidden.

Enjoying the freedom of being back with the fleet, Naomi Ward was wandering the halls of the Carrier winding down before the impending battle. She was also deep in thought about the events of the past weeks; the tough fighter pilot was certainly not the crying type. She had lost a good friend in Marks, but that wasn't going to knock her off her game. She had a job to do and if she could get some payback for her friend, then she was up for anything. She respected SC and was one of his closest friends, and knew her job was to back him up no matter what- which would always happen. It pleased her that he appreciated her enough to bring her in to the planning stages of the attack; it meant he trusted her, and she needed that reassurance at the moment. It was a tough time they were all experiencing. Because all anybody had was each other, that friendship bond that pulled them all together. Like Laverty, Naomi didn't agree with the military policy on fraternisation; that was old military, not new. Although she hadn't done anything about it yet, when the time came she knew she would, rules be damned: her reluctance up to this point was centred more around not finding the right guy. Despite everyone thinking her and Marks were a thing, they never crossed that boundary. The situation was a little irrelevant at the moment, as she reckoned she would unlikely meet anyone until they settled somewhere or were back on the Moon. *Smack!*

The next thing Ward knew was that she was lying flat on her back on the floor with the wind knocked out of her. She started sitting up slowly. looking around, she saw a similarly delirious and dishevelled looking man on the floor ahead of her. 'I'm so sorry!' he said looking straight at her.

'Wow!' Naomi said rubbing her head, 'what happened?'

'I was racing around that corner in my own world and I knocked you over, knocked both of us over,' replied the awkwardly handsome man that Naomi was now admiring. Slowly both of them got up, each a little dizzy from their encounter. 'It happens,' she replied, 'and to be honest I wasn't really paying attention either, so it's probably partly my fault, too.' Ward ran her fingers through her flowing hair, the hair grip she had it in had obviously been knocked out in the collision. She extended her other hand and introduced herself, 'Naomi Ward, Fire Starter pilot based on the Swan.'

'Geoff Wilson, head of Engineering, assigned to the Dreadnought, nice to meet you.'

Naomi and Geoff spoke on for a little while after their encounter before bidding each other good day and carrying on to their destinations; however, before she had gotten too far, a hand lightly gripped her arm. Turning around she was faced with a slightly out of breath engineer. 'Sorry,' he said, 'for troubling you again, but do you think, if we survive this raid that is, that you might want to meet up, and I would say get a drink, but as we have no alcohol aboard, maybe have a walk or a chat or something.'

It was evident that the engineer was nervous and as Naomi paused for a bit, she could see the fear in his eyes. Suddenly the fearless fighter pilot smiled, a beautiful smile which lit up her entire face and replied, 'I would love to.'

All crew members were ordered to return to their designated ships, with all non-essential personnel left aboard the Dreadnought. All ship systems were tested and retested; energy levels, shield power and weapons were set to maximum. The flight time would only take about two hours, and it was likely that they would be flying straight into a fire fight, so they wanted to ensure that all ships were completely ready before setting off. Travel speeds were synchronised as the entire fleet needed to arrive exactly at the same point: this in itself was a concern, as this had never been done before within the ERF, and now they were incorporating a number of different vessel configurations into the plan. The Fire Starters were all in the launch bays. With all the pre-launch checks carried out, the pilots would all mount their cockpits when the fleet was ten minutes from target.

Team assignments had been given out, what ships would partner with each other for the attack. Swan and Alexandra, Eagle and Valiant and O'Neil and Enterprise (with all that was going on, the Admiral had forgotten to rename the ship). SC's plan for Fire Starter distribution and tactics had been studied by all pilots and approved by the Admiral.

Everything and everybody was ready and prepared to go; after some words of luck coming from the Admiral, all seven ships set off at Overdrive to the Lambda System.

Chapter 8

The Lambda System is a small cluster of planets rotating around one sun, not too dissimilar from Earth's system. It was named in the same way as all the rest of the systems on the ERF's interstellar map; the USSF had designated them in much the same way as a list in a catalogue, meaning the names were uninspiring, but the system wasn't. It was the twelfth new area of space that the USSF had ventured into, and as they hadn't met any intelligent life by this point, they continued to designate systems phonetically. Lambda was seriously considered by the USSF for a human outpost, but to all available knowledge that plan had been abandoned due to the fact that the planet closest to Earth's habitability was a little closer to Venus distance from the sun, and not so much like Earth, which created a serious fear that any outpost setup there would deteriorate quickly in the heat and acidity of the planet.

What the USSF didn't realise at the time was it was at this point that they first encountered the Fedirian's, or more specifically, this was when the Fedirian's first noticed human beings. Hidden on the blindside of the third planets' moon was the very same Fedirian space station that the ERF were on their way to destroy.

This station was the Fedirian's most secretive high security space facility, though it was not entirely clear exactly what its function actually was. Trapped in constant nightfall, it never rotated into the sun's light, and is stably pitched in a hidden position to avoid detection from all space travellers. It would have remained hidden if not for two things: firstly, Haver accidentally unlocking the Enterprises restricted computer files, and secondly, the fleet of four Fedirian Heavy Cruisers circling around the moon.

The Fedirian forces had become aware of their not inconsiderable losses, making them very aware that they were being targeted. The best way for them to respond to this was to ensure that their best assets and facilities were secure, whilst compiling information on their enemy. The space station in the Lambda sector was of significant enough importance to the Fedirians that they would allocate four of their largest and most powerful ships to protect it.

The entire system was rigged with the minute sensors used to set the trap that the O'Neil fell in to when it discovered the Eagle, so that the second any ships entered the area they would be identified and the Cruisers would seek out and destroy them. The Fedirians were using this as a show of force, a reminder that they were not to be messed with under any circumstances. However, perhaps what they weren't expecting was a fleet of seven heavily armed ships and fifty fighters to arrive all at once.

Out of the darkness arrived the ERF fleet right inside the system, face to face with the enemy Cruisers. SC gave the order for all Fire Starters to launch on arrival; within two minutes the space was crowded with ERF fighters. The Fedirian Cruisers took up a defensive position and deployed a dozen fighter craft of their own, well below what the ERF were expecting. Taking up the agreed positions, the Dreadnought took up a static position at the back of the attacking fleet, aiming its mortar-style guns at the enemy ships. As soon as the fleet had moved into attacking position the Carrier fired its weapons. The Swan and the Alexandra were the first to engage, targeting the first Cruiser and opening fire. Although the enemy was returning fire, it was massively out gunned. The O'Neil was the next to engage, backed up by the Enterprise. They hammered into the second Cruiser with full firepower, the Cruiser, despite being well armoured and able to withstand a pounding, was struggling due to its lack of manoeuvrability, which was a bi-product of its size. An issue shared by the Eagle, who was trading punches head to head with the third Cruiser. Luckily, the Valiant, being more flexible with its movements, meant that it was harder to hit and able to dispense damage without receiving it.

The fifty attacking Fire Starters had the hardest job, tasked with engaging the dozen or so Fedirian fighters in the area, along with distracting the fourth Cruiser. Unfortunately, unlike the ease in which they were handling the enemy fighters, the thirty Fire-starters dedicated to attacking the Cruiser were having very little impact on its shields. Highlighting a weakness in the attacking fleet, the fourth Cruiser was targeting the Eagle with the majority of its firepower, meaning the large ex-USSF vessel was taking a pounding. The fourth Cruiser would have been ignoring the Fire Starters altogether had it not been for Speedy that seemed to be chipping away at its shields with seemingly stronger weaponry than the rest of the small ships.

SC and his usual wing person Karran were carrying out a series of hit and run drills on the Cruiser, weaving in and out of enemy fire, which all seemed to be concentrated on them. The upside of the firepower coming his way, thought SC, was that it was allowing Naomi the opportunity to lead a larger team to attack the Cruisers' engines. This was the primary goal: take out enemy ships engines and make it a sitting duck for whatever ERF ships finished with their ship first.

The Fedirians had made another fatal mistake in the conflict. As the Cruisers had come out to meet the ERF ships, they were out of the range of the powerful weapons of the space station. As a result they were completely on their own without support, a mistake the ERF had also made with the Dreadnought. By leaving the ship completely out of play it could not help in the conflict at all as now that the ships were all engaged together, the carrier couldn't risk firing its guns from afar for the fear of a friendly fire possibility. Luckily for the ERF the Swan was about to make a breakthrough.

After sustained assault from both the Swan and the Alexandra, the first Cruisers' shields had been lost and the thick armour had taken a pounding. Taking direction from Haver, the Swan concentrated firepower at a designated point around the middle of the enemy ship, breaking through to the central power core, eventually igniting the vessel and causing a ripple of explosions throughout. Beating a hasty retreat from the explosion, both the Swan and the Alexandra fled the doomed enemy ship, avoiding being engulfed in the explosion. Successfully destroying the first enemy combatant pushed the ERF fleet on to finish the battle, with the Swan engaging the fourth Cruiser alongside the fighters and the Alexandra joining the Valiant and Eagle to dispense with the third Cruiser.

The O'Neil was taking on heavy fire due to a malfunction with the Enterprises firing system, making it temporarily inoperable. Whilst repairs were being carried out Riley and the O'Neil were forced to hold off the second Cruiser alone. Despite the fact that they were breaking through the shields, they were having to manoeuvre heavily to try and avoid being hit, diminishing their ability to concentrate firepower.

'Jamieson, where is my back up?' Riley shouted through the comm.

'Coming Sir, the engineers think they are nearly there.' the new Captain replied.

'That's not the most reassuring answer I could have! Hurry up!' Responded the stressed Captain as he switched off the comm signal. 'Operations, find out if we can get any help over here at all!'

The call came over all the comm systems to support the O'Neil. SC picked it up and would have happily went to help; however, as it was only him and the Swan having any effect on the fourth Cruiser, he couldn't really justify leaving his post. However, he had just had a report that the enemy fighters had just been defeated. 'Smeaton, Whiterod and Santora, take the twenty Fire Starters who were engaged with the fighters and back up Riley with that second Cruiser. He just needs a little help until the Enterprise is back.' ordered SC through the comm.

The three pilots reported back to their Commander with a confirmation and proceeded to engage the second Cruiser with the help of twenty additional craft. Within a few minutes under the cover of the small fighters the Enterprise was back in play with a fully working targeting system they re-engaging the enemy ship. The benefit of having a three to one ratio on the third Cruiser meant that very shortly the enemy shipped bowed to the pressure of the assault and exploded in a massive fireball. The Eagle headed to where the second Cruiser was being assaulted and arrived to fire the final blow of that ships existence. Leaving the fourth Cruiser, weak from its entanglement with the many Fire Starters, Speedy, and the Swan, to be pummelled by the Valiant and the Alexandra as well. The last of the Cruisers did not last long under that bombardment and soon gave up the fight in a blaze of fire.

Although this was just an end to the first part of the fight, an uncontrollable cheer and applause erupted from every ship. For the first time since the majority of the residents came to space, they actually felt as though they were in the driving seat.

Before engaging with the space station, the fleet- except for the Dreadnought- grouped together to conduct a quick damage assessment. Although all ships had taken fire they were all in surprisingly good condition, with the exception of the Eagle that had incurred serious damage to all plating as the shields had been lost during the last encounter with the third Cruiser. The decision was made that it wasn't worth taking the risk of losing the big ship to have it attack the space station, as it would easily be picked out as the weak link. So the other five vessels would go it alone and the Eagle would make its way back toward the Dreadnought. Surprisingly all Fire Starters were still intact and none had been lost, so they would join the assault on the station.

The plan for this part was different, as they needed to disable the shields and the weapons but leave the infrastructure of the station intact in order to be boarded. As this was the key to Fedirian intelligence within the region, they would not get a better chance to understand their enemy than right now, so the plan had to work.

All ships took up an attack position, with assault teams being stationed on the Swan and Alexandra for the purpose of making a simultaneous assault on two entrances at the same time. The five ships and fifty Fire Starters entered weapons range and the space station opened all manner of hell upon the attacking ships, with plasma fire coming from at least fifty different points all at once. Luckily all the ERF ships were in good shape going in. With a significant amount of firepower themselves they could give as good as they got, the Fire Starters were able to weave around the plasma fire and deliver substantial punishment from a wide range of angles.

Although the station had strong shield power, the unrelenting bombardment of five ships and fifty small craft meant they could not stay up for long. The weapons systems control point was identified by Haver aboard the Swan, and the moment the shields fell it was obliterated by a concentrated burst of weapons fire from all craft, bringing a sudden silence to space all around. Cheers of joy could be heard on board all ships and through all the comm systems for the second time in the engagement, showing great relief from all the crew. However those in charge knew they were just about to engage in the most difficult part of the whole operation.

The Swan and Alexandra simultaneously moved into position and docked with the Fedirian space station on opposite sides. After the O'Neil's encounter with the 'Eagle' care was taken to ensure that no devices had been secured to the docking hatches which might cause damage to the attaching ships. The team from the Swan was led by Commander Hill, as normal, with Pillar as second in command, and the team from the Alexandra was led by Commander Chang, originally Chinese military, now a soldier of Earth in his eyes. His background was as an officer of the Chinese Army back on Earth and this seemed like a normal extension of his skill set. Both raiding parties gained access simultaneously and were met with gun fire the moment they set foot on the station. 'This is better,' thought Hill, smiling to himself. Although his raid on the other station and the ship had been relatively easier and safer, it never sat well with him to step on to an enemy combatant's ship without them attempting to repel him with force: at least he knew where he was with this response. Pillar, however, didn't quite agree with his superior's logic, longing for the quieter entrance.

Both teams advanced with only minor casualties being taken by the time they cleared the first corridor. Luckily no fatalities, but they had a long way to go to secure the entire station. Each raiding party hosted around sixty troops possessing significant firepower, which allowed each party the ability to break through enemy ranks Despite obviously fierce resistance, the enemy forces seemed unprepared for an assault of this magnitude. The Fedirian force were relying heavily upon automated defences to keep the invaders at bay; however lessons learned from the Enterprise helped equip the ERF soldiers on how to disable these defences quickly, as they knew they couldn't depend on having someone in the Control Centre this time. Implementing the drills practiced aboard the captured Fedirian ship, the raiding teams made short work of the defences, using their sporadic firing pattern against them. By use of armoured handheld shields to repel the occasional shot that fired their way, they were under the roof mounted turrets. What surprised the teams most during this stage of the attack was the lack of opposing soldiers for such a well-protected facility. If they had encountered more living resistance then the job of disarming the automated defences would have been considerably harder. Each team had encountered only a handful of Fedirian soldiers thus far and both assaults were approaching the command deck.

Both teams had been given the same destination, as it was agreed that rather than risk securing the entire base they could secure the routes to the Command Centre room itself, at least until the mission was complete. Hopefully this tactic would ensure a lesser demand upon the available troops, and so far so good, the strategy appeared to be working well. Hill's team were slightly ahead of Changs in relation to reaching their side of the Command deck; this was due mostly to how recently Hill's team had saw combat, meaning they had managed to get into a smoother rhythm working together to get through the defences. However, both teams had managed to avoid fatalities up to this point, so the tactics and the people were working well together.

Always leading from the front, Hill was the first to emerge onto the command deck of the station. Looking at the design, this could have been almost a carbon copy of the design of the Eagle's Command Centre, which he found strange as this was a space station, not a ship. The ageing Commander was slightly relieved to see the Command Centre was empty. Due to the toughness of the battle to get them there so far, he needed a respite; however, the last time he emerged onto an empty command deck there was a self-destruct set to go off, so the first move he made was to the central computer console to take a look for any countdown. It seemed clear; however, not being someone to leave anything to chance, he requested that one of his soldiers keep his eyes on the console at all times and to make him aware of any change to the display. The second team arrived and both worked together in unison to secure the deck. Within minutes they were as secure as they could be. The next challenge presented itself, in that, although experienced within some of the enemies systems, neither Hill or Chang had the knowledge required to download the content required from the stations database; so as soon as they were happy that the route and Command Centre was clear, Hill made the call back to the Swan. 'Captain, we are secure here for the moment, please send Haver along quickly.'

'Thank you Commander, and well done, he is on his way.' replied Captain Laverty.

Haver, along with half a dozen technical staff, made their way quickly out of the Swan's air lock and onto the enemy station. Rapidly moving along the corridors, they passed by a number of soldiers standing sentry in position, securing hatches from incursion. It took just a few minutes for Haver and his team to arrive on the command deck of the enemy station. Instantly, they began to get to work, the similarity of the Command Centre's layout to that of the Eagle made getting stuck into to the job easier as there was a higher degree of familiarity with the systems.

Hill was feeling the tension as he had accomplished his part of the assault and now the success of the mission was in someone else's hands. As much as he trusted his Operations Officer, he wanted to get finished and get off of the station before the situation changed. He just had a really uneasy feeling. Slowly, he wandered over to where Haver was working. 'Will this take long?' The older Officer inquired.

'Hard to say at the moment; we are downloading the whole memory core of the station and it's big. Also there are a couple of operational systems I'm not sure of here, and could do with someone else taking a look.' replied the young lieutenant.

'Who do you need? I'll get them for you.' responded Hill, desperate to do whatever he could to wrap up the operation as quickly as possible.

'If SC is available, he would be the best one to look at this.'

SC was in position close to the space station keeping a watchful eye over his Scanners. Having been bitten before with surprise attacks he was not willing to be taken unaware again. The call came through from Selina. 'SC, can you land on the Swan and proceed to the command deck of the station. Haver would like some assistance from you if possible.'

Tiring of his involvement upon enemy craft, SC really did not want to head on to another one. Just like Hill, he was desperate to finish the mission and head back to neutral space. Also, he was becoming unsure of how often he could keep putting himself in harm's way before he would get himself killed, but all of that was irrelevant: he is a good officer and if Haver needed him then he needed to go. 'Copy that Captain, heading in to the landing bay now.'

SC guided Speedy toward the rear of the Swan, arriving just as the landing bay doors finished opening. Careful as always, he landed his small craft in the designated space and quickly disembarked to make his way onto the enemy station.

In the meantime the Eagle had stopped mid-way between the fleet and the Dreadnought to affect a repair on the thruster system. Although the ship was built to take a beating, it was certainly showing the signs of the assaults it had incurred today and in the previous encounters. The Swan and Alexandra were both still attached to the station, constantly monitoring for activity aboard the enemy structure. The other three vessels, the O'Neil, Valiant and Enterprise formed a defensive perimeter around the station, on high alert, guarding against any surprises.

SC reached the command deck in double quick time, not wanting to prolong his stay aboard. Failing to stop for pleasantries, he galloped past the guards at the door and headed straight for Haver, 'Hey, what do you need?' He asked the Lieutenant.

'Hey, thanks for coming over,' smiled the young Lieutenant, 'we are downloading the information from the memory banks, but there is another system here that I need to find out whether or not there is anything in here that we need, but I don't understand what it is. They look like manoeuvring thrusters, which would make sense for the station, but with all the segways coming off of them they look far more complicated. You're more familiar with flight systems than I am, what do you think?'

'Let me take a closer look,' SC moved closer to the console and studied the Screen in front of him, 'A Space Station should not have half of these functions, thrusters are just for orbit positioning, I understand that this thing keeps a strange orbit but still, if I didn't know better I would say that these are full flight systems.' SC started looking around confused. He studied the command deck, 'Is it just me that thinks this looks like the Eagle?'

Hill, who had been listening to the exchange, was quick to respond, 'That's exactly what I thought when I first came in. That's strange, isn't it? It shouldn't have the same layout, should it? I know we all robbed the designs from the same people, but this is a space station, not a ship, and it's different from the Enterprise and the Swan, so it doesn't fit with the normal design.'

'I agree, it's strange, but we don't have time now to figure it out. Download the memory file from it anyway Baz, we may need it.' insisted SC.

Haver nodded, 'That's fine, this one is just finishing up now. I will start on it in just a second.'

Outside of the station, the Scanners on board all the ships started lighting, up with sirens going off all over the Command Centres. Those with any common sense had been expecting something; this included the Admiral, who was still stationed on-board the Dreadnought. Upon hearing the alarm he swiftly made his way to the Operations console where the ship's Captain was already standing studying the monitor, 'What do we have?'

Captain Hatherly looked up from his monitor and responded with a fearful look in his eyes, 'Six enemy ships incoming, three Cruisers and three destroyers.'

Panic struck in the Admirals eyes, 'Where are they Captain? How far out?'

'They are here sir.' Hatherly replied quickly, the fear consuming him almost completely.

The Admiral started to look annoyed, responding sharply, 'What do you mean by "here", Captain?'

Hatherly pointed upwards before muttering, 'Right on top of us!'

Chapter 9

Hatherly wasn't kidding when he said that the Fedirians were on top of them; all six ships had come out of overdrive strategically surrounding the carrier. Moving into position, all ships opened fire immediately. The one fortunate circumstance was that the Dreadnought had been battle ready; its shields were fully raised and able to intercept the firepower of the attacking crafts. The ten Fire Starters that were in defensive positions around the carrier immediately concentrated their attack on the nearest destroyer, knowing full well that they had little chance of harming a fully armed cruiser; the smaller fighter squadron could aim only to weaken the smaller of the two types of heavily armed ships.

Being the closest to the Dreadnought the Eagle scrambled to support the surrounded and vulnerable carrier; however, due to its earlier battle damage, they had only been able to restore minimal shields and would quickly fall into trouble unless backup was received soon. All hands near the space station were called to alert and hurriedly made their way towards the attacking fleet surrounding the Dreadnought. Forty nine Fire Starters, the Valiant, the O'Neil and the Enterprise all set course for the large enemy fleet. The Alexandra detached from the station, leaving the Swan to recover all the soldiers on board.

Laverty sounded a general recall for all troops to return to the Swan so that it could participate in the defence of the Carrier. Unfortunately for Selina the soldiers on board the station weren't quite ready to leave.

'We need to go now!' Bellowed Hill, who was towering above the much shorter officer.

'I'm not finished yet, I need more time.' pleaded Haver.

'Baz, we don't have time, we are sitting ducks here whilst the fleet is engaged with the enemy. We need to get out of here and back on the Swan to re-join them so we can assist with holding the enemy off!' Shouted SC, who was now wanting to leave more than anything and worried that his earlier prophecy of dying on an enemy station was about to come true.

'I need two more minutes then I'll be done, 'Haver looked at SC pleadingly, 'Come on, it'll take longer than that to get the troops back aboard the Swan.' insisted the young Lieutenant.

'Let's do that then, Commander,' offered SC reluctantly, 'get all the troops back on board, I will stay with Haver and then we will double time it to the ship the second he is done.'

'If you two are going to be stupid enough to carry on then I'm staying too!' stated Hill, 'Pillar, get everyone back to the Swan now!'

'Yes Sir,' responded the younger soldier respectfully, who was quietly happy that he would soon be off this hostile station, although heading straight into a fire fight with more hostile ships probably wasn't much better, he thought to himself.

Soldiers quickly started peeling off from their posts as others passed them in a scramble, Havers technical team accompanying Pillar back toward the ship at a fast pace, leaving just Hill, SC and the increasingly more unpopular Lieutenant who was hurriedly transferring files. He could detect the feeling of eyes peering into the back of his head, making him work faster.

'Your two minutes are just about up, Lieutenant!' Shouted Hill, 'We really need to go. I have had word that the rest of the troops are back aboard the Swan.'

'Just a little longer!' Yelled Haver, knowing he would probably pay for that insubordination later.

At that moment the hatches on the command deck closed and sealed, 'Eh, what's going on?' asked SC in a confused tone.

'The hatch is sealed,' responded Hill who was pulling at the door like a madman. 'We are locked in!'

The central computer console lit up with declining numbers, 180, 179, 178......

'I don't wish to alarm anybody, but it would seem that the self-destruct is active.' exclaimed Haver.

'We are trapped!' Shouted Hill.

The three men looked at each other for a few seconds in disbelief, then the sudden realisation set it that they didn't have long left and they needed to act fast. 'Can we override the door?' ventured SC.

'Unlikely; it's a defence mechanism, designed to lock us out from the outer rim during self-destruct. It would take too long to work around it.' Haver replied.

'And it takes the best part of three minutes to get back to the ship anyway.' stated a resigned Hill.

SC nodded at Hill, accepting the point that the older officer was making. Speaking softly, yet determinedly, into his comm unit 'Captain, you need to break off immediately: this station is about to blow.'

'Are you almost back on board? Where are you?' Responded Laverty.

'We aren't going to make it back, we are still aboard the station and the Command Centre has sealed us in. We are stuck, you need to go now, there's no time.' replied the Lt Commander resolutely.

'That's not acceptable SC, we will send a cutting team over to get you out.' The Captain ordered.

'Damn it Selina, listen to me, there is no time, we only have two minutes left.' shouted the distraught pilot.

'We can't just leave you!' protested Laverty, tears forming in her eyes.

'You need too.' instructed the doomed officer.

The decision was taken out of Selina's hands as another Fedirian Cruiser arrived, this one right next to the space station. Due to the position of the floating structure, the enemy ship couldn't immediately get a weapon lock on the Swan, giving the ERF ship enough time to disconnect from the station and raise shields. If Selina was going to lose SC, Hill and Haver, she would make sure she took the enemy with her. Setting weapons to maximum, the Swan engaged the Cruiser head on.

Meanwhile on the command deck of the station, '110, 109, 108...'

Something was bothering SC, 'Why would the doors seal?'

'To stop us escaping.' answered Hill.

'That doesn't make sense though, three minutes isn't really enough time to escape and why lock us in? The computer wouldn't know it was us, they wouldn't expect it to be enemy combatants within the command deck, how would the Fedirian's get out if they had set it from here?' contributed Haver.

Suddenly the dots began to join, 'Unless we are already in the escape route!' Exclaimed SC. 'We said there seemed to be flight controls, maybe the command deck separates from the rest of the station.'

'Quick!' shouted Hill, 'we don't have much time.'

The Swan was playing a good game of attack and evade, exploiting the benefits of a more manoeuvrable craft, although when the Cruiser did land hits on the ERF ship, the shields took a pounding. Selina could only hope that the damage they were doing was hurting the Fedirian vessel more. Time had gotten away from her and she was concentrating so hard on defeating the ship in front of her she didn't think about the three stranded men aboard the Space station.

The Eagle and the Dreadnought were in bad shape, the Eagle having taken extensive damage in the earlier battle and the Dreadnought taking a pounding in the opening salvo of the counter-attack. The Enterprise was the first support vessel to arrive and assist the two vulnerable vessels; the Fedirians were obviously so angry to be fighting against one of their own ships that they altered their attack pattern and bombarded it with plasma fire as soon as it entered weapons range. The only upside to this was that the arrival of the Enterprise took immediate pressure off of the other two ERF vessels. Soon afterwards the Valiant and O'Neil arrived, with forty nine Fire Starters ready to join the fight, the Alexandra following close behind.

This part of the attack was unplanned and as a result all of the ERF ships were behaving responsively rather than co-operatively, causing them to all target different vessels. Only the Fire Starters were holding it together, with Ward ordering them to join with the existing ten small craft in attacking a destroyer. Suddenly the annoying blasts of ten small fighters became the roar of fifty nine Fire Starters pulverising the destroyers' shield system. The Dreadnought's shields were starting to fail, the Eagle had lost the little shields it had and was unable to withstand much more bombardment despite the arrival of reinforcements. The survival of the stricken ships was looking unlikely.

59, 58, 57..... Went the countdown clock on the space station, Haver, Hill and SC were running around like wild men trying to operate systems designed for five between the three of them. 'We need to go now, Baz!' demanded SC.

Haver raised his arms up defensively for a second, in a back off type motion, 'I just need to release the docking clamps, then we can go.'

'Release them now, otherwise there won't be any docking clamps to release.' shouted SC.

The Swan was taking heavy damage from the Fedirian Cruiser; the evading action wasn't nearly as effective as it had been, the assaulting craft finally finding its mark with around thirty percent of its shots. The Captain knew she needed to do something different if she was to destroy the larger vessel, 'Draw them in closer to the station,' commanded Selina, 'if that's going to go then maybe we will get lucky and it can take them too.'

The Swan cut in close to the station to draw the pursuing ship nearer to the imminent explosion, the Fedirian Cruiser, obviously unaware of the timescale of the explosion, followed the exact path of the ERF vessel. Selina tried to contact SC on the comm unit as the explosion time drew closer, attempting to say a final goodbye, but there was no answer, so she steeled herself to the inevitable occurrence. Moments later the space station exploded, the blast so powerful it swept the Swan off of its course. The flames engulfed the Cruiser and although it survived the blast, its shields were down and it had incurred massive damage.

The force of the shockwave temporarily knocked out the Swans targeting Scanners, causing a similar effect upon the Fedirian vessel too. Unable to lock on to a target, the Swans crew were working manically to re-engage the system. The Fedirian vessel, however, had started to fire wildly. Without being able to lock on to a target they were just estimating where the ERF ship was and attempted to blindly hit it. The first twenty or so shots went nowhere; however, they were closing in on the target. The Swan's engineers reported that they would need a few minutes to re-initialise the system, which normally wouldn't have been an issue, but the engines had stalled too, and the Swan was a sitting duck. At least until they could target their weapons.

The Fedirian Cruiser finally had a hit. They clipped the shields of the Swan with a blind shot which was enough to allow them to take a bearing from the impact, allowing the enemy to partially target the ship. By re-aiming at that general area of space, the cruiser opened up another volley of plasma fire, with sixty percent of the shots finding their target. The Swan was shaking with every hit, the shields were failing, and consoles were exploding all over the ship. If something didn't change soon there was no way they would survive. Captain Laverty was normally good at finding a way through difficult situations, however without engines and targeting Scanners, she was at a loss of how to save her crew.

Out of the wake and wreckage of the station arose a great and powerful looking vessel. It was a strange configuration and considerably larger than even the Fedirian Cruisers: a central structure with three arms coming forward from the rear, hosting multiple forward pointing blasters. The ship rotated around, focused all of its considerable weapons at the cruiser attacking the Swan, and unleashed more firepower than anyone present had ever witnessed. The Cruisers' weakened state meant it was incapable of withstanding any real damage, and promptly exploded into countless pieces of wreckage.

'What the hell was that?' yelled Laverty with an expression of relief. The response that came through the comm unit was not what Selina expected, 'Lt Commander Cave, Commander Hill and Lieutenant Haver reporting for duty, Captain.'

'It took you long enough, Lt Commander,' replied the Captain smiling, ' you can explain this to me later: the fleet needs you, can you assist whilst we make some quick repairs?'

'Roger that, Captain.' replied SC.

'Oh, and Lt Commander. Welcome back.'

The situation with the fleet had turned grave: the Dreadnought was limping its way out of battle in an attempt to prolong its own survival, followed closely by the Eagle, which had gaping holes straight through the ship, looking like it was in dire need of a space dock for repairs. Still engaged with the enemy were the entire compliment of Fire-starters along with the Enterprise, the O'Neil, the Alexandra and the Valiant. The enemy had lost one destroyer; however, the other five attacking ships remained.

'Riley to the Dreadnought. Admiral, what are your orders?' The O'Neil's Captain needed to change the run of play, he knew they needed a plan.

'This is Sharp, first officer of the Dreadnought, all ships, the Admiral is dead, the vice Admiral and Captain Hatherly are critical, we have no functioning leadership. We have a reactor leak and I have the engineers locked in at the moment trying to contain it. Sorry Captains, it's down to you, we are out of this fight, we are no use to anyone.'

The news of the death of the Admiral echoed throughout the fleet; unfortunately, due to the blazing fire fight all around them there was no time to pause and grieve. A definite flaw was realised in the organisation of the fleet, in event that the Admiral and Vice Admiral were incapacitated, command would fall to the Captain of the Flagship. In this case that meant Hatherly. As he was also out of commission, it should really fall to his replacement. However, Sharp was a relatively inexperienced second in command and had more than enough on his hands protecting his ship from destruction. Command had never been as unclear as it was right now. 'This is Riley to all ships: we need a plan, carry on or bug out, we aren't making any progress like this.'

The comm system was silent, it seemed as though nobody was willing to make a decision or a declaration that could influence the entire fleet. In reality, despite that there were a number of Captains in the fleet, none of them had seen combat like this. Even taking into account that they all came from a military background, hard combat was a novelty and they were more inclined to take orders rather than give them. Eventually, after what seemed like an eternity-in truth it was more like one minute- a voice broke through, 'This is SC aboard the Liberator, all ships target the Cruiser furthest to the left; its shields are weakest and it looks like a concentrated effort could take it quickly. Fire

Starters, continue the barrage on the second destroyer, you are breaking through. We are targeting the third destroyer, in about one minute we should turn the tide of this assault.'

After a moment of silence and confusion, all parties followed the instructions from the new ship. Despite SC being a lower ranked officer, he was a man with a plan, which is what was needed at this point. All ships very quickly turned their fire towards the new targets and unleashed all of their fury upon the two ships identified whilst the Liberator hammered the third destroyer. Ninety seconds later, almost simultaneously, there were three explosions in space, leaving two Fedirian Cruisers still healthy and still attacking despite suddenly being very vulnerable. SC then re-organised the fleet into a new pattern having the four ERF vessels attacking one Cruiser, and the Liberator coordinating an assault with the aid of the full complement of Fire Starters on the other Cruiser.

Undoubtedly, the firepower of the Liberator was far more impressive than any other vessel, and as such it was making short work of the Cruiser it was attacking. SC and his mighty craft were joined shortly after engaging by the Swan, adding to the force being impacted upon the enemy vessel that was quickly showing signs of buckling. The other ships were doing well to subdue the other Fedirian Cruiser that they were targeting; however, nobody had realised quite how much damage the Enterprise had taken during the early part of the fight, and then again during the group assaults, especially with most of the enemy assault focusing on the captured vessel. Against the current run of play the unexpected happened, the Enterprise exploded without announcement or warning: it just vanished in a flash of fire and light.

Without stopping to question what had happened, the remaining vessels continued to pound their targets, knowing there would be time for grieving later. The cruisers attempted to fight back, taking the destruction of the Enterprise as an opportunity to turn the tide, but the intense firepower from the sheer number of weapons targeting them became far too much for either ships' defences to handle, resulting in two brilliant explosions right in front of the ERF fleet. There was almost a sense of disbelief throughout all the Command Centres' on board all of the ships. The battle was over, the ERF had won, but for now, there was no telling how much they had lost.

Chapter 10

'All ships, damage report.' requested SC through the comm system.

'O'Neil, low shield power but overall no extensive damage.' came Riley's reply. Despite the heavy fire power on display, the O'Neil's manoeuvrability had ensured that they avoided the majority of plasma damage.

'Valiant: minor hull damage, no shields but all other systems functioning.' After the destruction of the Enterprise, the Valiant took a lot of abuse from the Cruiser. Luckily they destroyed the ship before taking on any real damage.

'Alexandra: Command Centre inoperable, however ship is still functional, no shields.' The shields on the Alexandra had fallen during the last volley of fire, and due to its proximity to the exploding cruiser the already weak hull surrounding the command Centre gave way. Luckily the Captain realised the issue was about to occur prior to the event and gave the order to evacuate just in time.

'Swan: partial engine damage, shields at minimum power, but all other systems operating within normal perimeters.' The Swan had affected a repair to get weapons targeting and engines back online before re-joining the Liberator in battle. Luckily the cruiser failed to see them as the biggest threat, so fundamentally left them alone during the final exchange.

'Eagle: severe damage to all systems, large gaping holes in the middle of the ship. Will take days to secure it for travel.' Standing in front of the Dreadnought as a punching bag meant that the already vulnerable Eagle incurred massive damage from all six attacking ships. Its survival was a testament to the sturdiness of the design, combined with the enemy aggressors' inability to hit anything too sensitive.

'Dreadnought: massive damage, major reactor leak, only life support and thrusters currently functioning. Half of the Command Centre has been destroyed. We need some assistance; our engineers are under equipped to deal with the severity of the issues.' The Dreadnought, despite being a large and well armoured ship, had had to cope with a six ship bombardment. The size of the vessel meant that it was unable to avoid any hits and its shields had almost collapsed by the time the Eagle had arrived to assist.

'What is the status of Commander Wilson?' Asked SC, knowing that the head of fleet engineering was aboard the Dreadnought.

The reply came quickly from the Dreadnoughts first officer, 'Wilson is in with the reactor, but he has been in too long, we need to pull him out; we need more engineers trained in this type of repair so we can change over.'

The Swan and the Valiant quickly docked with the Dreadnought whilst they transferred personnel to assist with the repair. It was apparent that everyone was tired. However, SC still couldn't allow the crews to rest, not knowing if any more visitors might be in-bound. Spare engineering staff were also transferred to the Eagle to assist with repairs. Special consideration was being paid to repairing the engines on all ships, in an attempt to get the fleet mobile enough to move to another system for safety. In the meantime, the Fire Starters were organised into a defensive pattern, with the exhausted pilots acting as a quick response team for any potential attacks. From the command deck of the Liberator, Haver had managed to take control of the Fedirian sensor net in order to be able to detect incoming ships from outside the ERF's Scanner range.

Although the Captains and Commanders of the fleet needed to debrief, it was decided that this needed to wait until the fleet could move to a safer position. So, for the following six hours, all crew members worked exhaustively to ensure that their ships were ready to move, attack or defend at a moment's notice. Eventually, the reactor leak aboard the Dreadnought was contained and the engines repaired upon the Eagle. None of the two worst effected ships were really fit to travel; however, the risk of remaining in their current position was too great. All seven ships set off into overdrive for around half an hour to a pre-arranged rendezvous point. The rendezvous was deemed to be far enough from the Lambda system to allow the ERF to regroup, debrief and conduct repairs without fear of interruption. As an extra protection, the fleet formed up behind the moon of a large gas giant with the hope that they should be protected from any onlookers.

The Swan was the first ship to dock with the Liberator and Selina raced quickly out of the hatch and into SC's arms. For a minute all they did was hold each other, before she backed off slightly from the embrace, but not entirely letting him go. 'What happened?' It seemed strange that this was the first time this question had been asked, but due to the dramatic turn of events and the hurried repairs, this was the first opportunity to really speak since the space station exploded.

SC took a minute to think, it was evident that he was trying to find the best way to explain the situation himself. 'It turns out that the entire station was built around this ship. We didn't realise it at first and the Fedirian's had hidden the details of it in the computer banks, so despite using it for our escape, it wasn't until the last few hours that we have actually learned what we were piloting. The piloting controls on the command deck was the first give away that it might be a ship, that combined with the most complicated manoeuvring thruster set up ever to be seen on a space station. Once we realised we might be able to detach the ship we set about doing just that. Take it from me that was one hectic three minutes.'

'What happened when it exploded, did you detach in time? We didn't see you.' responded a still flustered Laverty.

'Once the docking clamps detached, we had about thirty seconds to go. The design of the station meant that we had to reverse out of the docking ring. We had literally just cleared the rim when it exploded; luckily, Hill had gotten the shields up and prevented our destruction. The shockwave sent us into the gravitational pull of the moon. Once we stabilised the controls and our orbit we were able to break free and come up to assist.'

'You have nine lives, you know that?' Laughed a very happy Selina.

All of the other ship Captains reported to the Liberator, all desperate for a look at the newly captured Fedirian ship, which was infinitely more impressive than the Enterprise had been. SC waited for all the Captains to be seated. Joining them were Commander Hill and Lieutenant Ward. 'Thanks everyone for coming over, I understand you were all itching for a look at the Liberator, I think you will agree that she is an impressive ship. Before we continue, I have invited Lieutenant Ward and Commander Hill into this debrief as for half of the attack Ward was in command of the Fire Starters, and Hill took command of the space station raid. Any questions before we begin?'

SC looked around the room at the senior officers he was largely faced with. Everyone seemed relatively expressionless until Clarke raised his hand, 'I have a question.'

'Please,, go ahead.' answered SC.

'Why are you in charge? Not of the meeting, I get that: your ship, your table- but the Liberator? I mean no disrespect to anyone here, but Commander Hill outranks you. Why are you in charge?' It seemed as though Clarke was not attempting to be difficult but he obviously wanted to clarify an issue that everyone was thinking about.

'Captain, if I may, I believe I am best to answer this question.' replied Hill, 'You are correct, my rank does make me senior to the Lt Commander: However, it never entered my mind to override him on this at any point. I have served with SC for over a year. While it's certainly true that we haven't always agreed on the best way to do things, I have faith in his ability. The Admiral sent him on a suicide mission less than a week ago, and I knew if anyone could find a way to succeed it would be him, and when we were on that station with only three minutes to live it was him that found our way out. I'm not saying he did it single handedly, Haver did a fantastic job and I played my part in operating the systems, but it was SC that got us out of there. I am an experienced leader of soldiers, but when it comes to tactical space battles and problem solving, I will happily take my lead from him. I would also state that he has saved my life on numerous occasions, and if it hadn't been for SC the majority of us wouldn't be here now.'

SC felt it almost impossible to stop a smile reaching his lips. He visibly blushed as he absorbed the kind words that had just been spoken about him, and it was a feeling of deep pride to know that he was well thought of, despite all that had just been said. However, he couldn't have been prepared for what happened next.

'Thank you Commander,' stated Clarke smiling, 'I wasn't questioning his suitability to command, and I agree with you that the Lt Commander was influential in the survival of so much of the fleet. I just wanted to understand what had happened and as such before we move on to larger concerns I would like to propose that SC be promoted to the rank of acting Captain of the Liberator, pending review by the Vice Admiral when he regains consciousness.

The verdict was unanimous, with all parties, including Ward, whose vote didn't entirely count, agreeing that SC should be given his own command. After the vote the conversation turned to the condition of Lewis and Hatherly, the verdict being that they were both critical and suffering with head injuries. Their injuries were the result of the explosion of the centre console on the command deck of the Dreadnought. The Admiral had absorbed the full force of the explosion with the shockwave knocking the other two senior officers head first into wall mounted computers. The ship's doctor had placed both men into comas in order to give their brains a chance to heal, and would be monitoring them steadily.

The next item on the agenda was the condition of the fleet. The loss of the Enterprise and her crew had hurt the ERF; the only consolation was that it had been staffed with minimal manpower due to the simplicity of its operation. Meaning in total the losses incurred with its destruction were twelve souls. Combined with the casualties on the other ships, the ERF had lost around forty people with another fifty four in serious condition and a few hundred with cuts and bruises. All in all they had survived the conflict well. However, the ships themselves were a different story; the Liberator was in good condition, minor damage that would be easily repaired, the Valiant and the Alexandra needed a couple of days intensive repair and they would be back at full strength, the O'Neil and the Swan were in need of a days-worth of tender loving care and they would be back to top condition. The Eagle and the Dreadnought were a different story altogether: the Eagle was by far the worst. It needed a space dock in order to effect proper repairs. They could patch it for the moment, but it would be unlikely to survive another attack. The Dreadnought needed serious repairs, two month-worth of repair work was required unless they had access to a space dock then they could do the work in around two weeks.

It was decided that they should meet back together in one day, in order to get a full picture of what was needed. Those ships that could be repaired easily would be, those that couldn't would provide a realistic assessment on requirement. For security purposes, Ward would organise a defensive patrol using her fleet of Fire Starters, allowing some of them to rest whilst the others patrolled and then swap them out. Just as the group was starting to disperse SC stopped Commander Sharp, 'oh how is Wilson doing?'

Hearing the name Ward turned around quickly, 'What do you mean? What's going on with Wilson?'

Sharp was slightly on edge with Wards' reaction, 'Erm, well, he fixed the leak in the reactor, but he took on a dangerous amount of radiation doing it. He is stable at the moment, but it is unlikely he will improve. He saved the ship, in all honesty, but he probably killed himself doing it.'

Naomi's face was one of complete shock. She knew she didn't know him very well, but having lost a good friend in Marks just a couple of weeks earlier, and now someone that she had felt a connection with, it was all getting to be too much, 'Commander do you mind if I come aboard to see him?'

'Of course, please, come with me.' responded Sharp.

SC couldn't help but be surprised by his friends' reaction to the situation. He wasn't aware that the head of engineering and Ward even knew each other. He liked Wilson, they had attended a few senior staff meetings together and he seemed to be a good guy. It would be a real shame to lose such a nice person and a great asset to the fleet.

The day passed very quickly, with engineering teams working around the clock to make repairs on all the easily repairable ships, ensuring a team of well armoured defenders to look after the rest of the vulnerable fleet. Before the next meeting the Swan and the O'Neil were back to combat ready condition with the Alexandra not far behind. The team had hit a small snag with the repairs to the Valiant, with a few systems shorting out due to fused wiring that they hadn't spotted before. However, it seemed likely that they could have it sorted within a day and a half. The Eagle and the Dreadnought had achieved little more than an inspection, which produced a long list of repairs needing to be completed. The systems were made safe, but the repairs on these ships would be a massive undertaking.

Ward spent the majority of the next twenty four hours at Wilson's bedside. Although he was unconscious, she was doing her best to remind him of their vaguely planned date, letting him know that a little radiation poisoning wasn't enough to excuse him from the arrangement they had made. When it was time to head to the meeting with senior staff she couldn't believe how much time had passed. Along with the rest of the ships' senior staff, she made her way to the Liberator to find out what the next stage of the plan was.

After all parties gathered and pleasantries had been exchanged, the senior officers reported on the condition of the ships one day on. Hearing that the Eagle and the Dreadnought were in such bad condition didn't enthuse anyone and made it unclear as to what the next action should be. Ward reported on the worsening condition of the fleet's head of engineering, putting it in no uncertain terms that unless action was taken he would not survive.

'What action could we possibly take?' Asked Taylor, who had remained relatively quiet until now.

'We used to have advanced medical devices that could reverse the effects of radiation poisoning. What has happened to them?' Queried a frustrated Ward.

Everyone at the table looked around at each other with expressions of confusion; evidently this was the first time a matter such as this had been brought to this group. Although most of the officers knew that these devices existed, they had no idea as to where they were. Again, it was Clarke that brought his voice to the situation, 'They were left on the moon; we had them in the medical centre. It was always the intention to have them on board the larger ships eventually, but we were caught by surprise and the majority of medical devices and supplies never made it aboard.'

Naomi's head dropped and tears began filling her eyes, 'So that means they are lost then, and so is Wilson.'

'I'm afraid so.' followed up Clarke.

SC, who had remained suspiciously quiet up until this point, raised his head and joined the conversation, 'Unless they aren't.'

All eyes landed on the new Captain. Riley, who already had some idea of what his old friend had in mind, was the first to speak, 'What do you mean?'

SC considered his response for a moment. 'It's no secret that I was an advocate for going back to Earth, or at least the Solar System. I suspected that there is a chance that we still have people alive and well on the Moon. Combined with the fact that from what intelligence suggests, the Fedirians are weaker now than they have ever been, gives us the best opportunity to take back our home. I am not saying let's go back just for Wilson, but there is also a chance that if we are able to go back and remove the opposition, we could salvage the shipyards on the moon to effect repairs and add to our fleet. I'm not saying it's going to be easy, but it's a possibility, and it means we could go home, or at least close to home.'

The room were a little stunned by the suggestion and although Naomi knew this wasn't all about Wilson, she was wondering if her friendship with SC had partly pushed him there. It was Captain Clarke who responded, 'SC, I like the sentiment, but putting aside the complications of defeating an enemy fleet whilst we aren't exactly fighting fit ourselves, the shipyards on the moon were the first things to get hit in the attack a year ago. It's unlikely there would be anything left to salvage.'

Around the table Clarkes' comment was causing a chorus of nodding heads. SC began to feel a little dismayed at the lack of support for his plan.

'We could always use the Mars shipyard.' suggested Derek.

Surprise and confusion swept around the table at the Eagle Captain's remark. 'Sorry Derek, you mustn't have known the Mars shipyards were destroyed during the initial invasion.' replied Riley.

'I was on Mars when the invasion started; the surface ship yards were destroyed, not the subterranean one,' responded Derek.

Yet again the room was left dumbstruck, this time staring at Derek Strong. 'What subterranean shipyard?' Questioned a confused Riley.

'There was an underground cavern, discovered not long after the base was constructed, so the decision was made to build an extra yard for black ops missions and vessels. When the base was hit in the opening attack, we powered it down to avoid detection, the idea being that we would return after we secured Earth. When the battle was sure to be lost, all ships fled for their own survival, and we had to leave the Mars project behind.'

This news was like a bombshell to the rest of the group, even Riley, who was a member of the USSF at that time and had no knowledge of this. However, it occurred to him, as he was a relatively low ranking officer it was entirely conceivable that this was above his pay grade. 'How can we be sure that the base is still intact? Would they even have enough supplies to last this long'? Asked Clarke.

'We can't be sure but we have no reason to think it isn't. As for supplies, it was the US military, of course we stocked for like, ten years at a time.' answered Derek jovially.

'How many people did you leave behind?' Asked SC.

'About nine hundred people or so, if I remember correctly.' replied the Eagle's Captain.

'Nine hundred people?' Questioned a bewildered SC.

'Around that, more or less.' responded the ex USSF Captain.

'That sells it for me,' SC stated categorically, 'we need a plan for going back.'

Up until now most in the room had been sitting quietly thinking of ways to disagree with more offensive action; now they were faced with the all-new information that they weren't the only ones still alive, and there were a lot more people living in a secret base next door to the planet they used to call home. What made it worse was the realisation that they were all living so closely while they were on the Moon. Clarke was still unconvinced of the viability of the idea, 'I agree that the fact there are people alive back there is compelling and I know we need the facilities, but how do we get around the fact that we are heavily outgunned within the region? Especially with two of our heavy hitters in tragically bad shape, and of course we don't know for certain that everything we need is still there!'

'Nobody said we had to announce our presence;' replied SC, 'if we were to send an individual ship into the area, we could approach Mars stealthily and ascertain the situation within the region and on Mars. If it's viable then the one ship could open the door for the remainder of the fleet.'

'Just who are you thinking should go?' Asked Clarke.

SC smiled and responded, 'I'm happy to go with the Liberator,' responded the confident new Captain, 'She can be piloted with a minimal crew and has enough firepower to put up a fight if we are discovered. An obvious choice, I would think.'

Something had been bugging Riley up until now and he wanted get it out there: 'Can we be sure that the Liberator won't give out some kind of signal when it is in the proximity of other Fedirian vessels? It is their ship, after all.'

'Actually, it's not,' SC replied, 'Haver accessed the records on the ship just this morning. It turns out that the Fedirians acquired the vessel adrift with no crew aboard around thirty years ago. They boarded it, but it refused to work for them; the computers would not give them access to the flight controls or weapons. So, unwilling to let it go at that, the Fedirians constructed a space station around it. Hiding it from anyone who may come looking, taking time to study the design and weapons systems to try and reverse engineer them, whilst also trying to break through the ship's security to make it functional for them.'

'So how did you and Haver get it running in three minutes when the Fedirian's couldn't in thirty years?' Asked Riley.

'I'm not sure we did,' answered SC, 'I think the ship did it.'

'What do you mean?' Requested Clarke.

'Either the ship detected it was in danger of being destroyed and saved itself, or it realised we weren't a threat and let us have access. Whatever the reason, the ship is working now and it's working for us.' answered the alien ship's new Captain.

'That would suggest some sort of Artificial Intelligence built into the ship.' stated Selina.

'I think so.' responded SC. 'Whatever the reasons are that we have access, I have no idea, but what I do know is that it is the most powerful ship we have ever came into contact with and it's ours, which makes it the only good option for a mission to Mars.'

Although unhappy about going against SC, Selina still had concerns. 'If the Liberator does have an AI, what's to stop it shutting down on you if you take into battle again?'

'It didn't have to save us before, but it did. I can only think that there is some history between the ship builders and the Fedirians, and maybe it was programmed not to respond to them; I don't know for certain, but here is the thing, when you fly her she feels like she wants to help, everything about her is geared for battle.' responded SC.

'Do you have any information on who the ship builders are?' Asked Clarke.

'Unfortunately not, according to the data logs the Fedirians never ascertained the ship's origin.'

'We are wasting time!' Yelled Ward. 'I am sorry for my outburst, but does it matter at the moment? Geoff is laying in critical condition; so are Lewis and Hatherly. We need better medical facilities and we know where to go to get them. Can't the rest of this wait? We have lives that are hanging in the balance.'

'We understand that, Commander,' replied Riley, 'but we have to be sure about our actions or even more lives could be in danger.'

SC stood up, looked over at Naomi and nodded, turning to the rest of the group he stated, 'I would like to move forward with a plan to take the Liberator to Mars, to ascertain what assets we have available. I also suggest taking Wilson with me so that if we are in a position to help him we can do so quickly. I doubt back up will be required; however, I am happy to take Commander Ward's squadron of Fire Starters with me, and before Captain Laverty says anything, I would also like the Swan to base itself close to the edge of the system, but out of detector range, just in case we need help. What do you think of that?'

Nodding around the room indicated that there was a consensus; the plan was quickly agreed on and preparations were started, with all relevant ships and manpower being moved to the Liberator. SC had insisted upon a small crew along with a tactical unit, not wanting to take any unnecessary risks to personnel. Wilson was transported in to the medical bay of the Liberator with the Fire Starters- along with Speedy- being moved into the hangar bay. The fleet status was set to high alert, with the remaining ships forming a defensive barrier around the damaged vessels. The Liberator and the Swan detached themselves from the remaining fleet and set their course for the Milky Way. Riley offered some parting words across the comm system, 'Good luck out there guys, and find your way back soon.'

'Copy that my good friend, stay safe and we will be back before you know it.' replied SC.

With that parting shot, both ships took off at Overdrive heading for Earth and an unknown situation, clouded by theories, beliefs and memories of what remained.

Chapter 11

Stopping just outside the Solar System the Liberator and the Swan both carried out scans of the region. Detecting no immediate movement or enemy ships was what would give SC the confidence to proceed with the plan. Having learned from previous encounters, SC ensured that they scanned for trip wire signals or early detectors, anything that might give away the stealthy entrance they needed to make. 'All scans are clear, Captain.' acknowledged Haver.

'Keep actively scanning for anything, it doesn't make sense that there is nothing, unless they are doing something different.' Responded SC. Activating the comm unit, SC continued, 'Selina, we are going to move in; watch our back and I will let you know as soon as I have any information.'

'You take care Captain; we will be monitoring your progress. At even the slightest hint of weapons fire we will be following you in.' replied his former Captain.

SC smiled to himself and responded, 'Understood.'

Taking all relevant care, the Liberator made its way into the Solar System, keeping in close proximity to planets to mask its signal from scanning enemy ships. SC had his crew constantly monitoring the space all around them for trip signals or small ships that could expose their approach.

Although SC and his crew could detect activity within the system, it was obvious that they hadn't yet been spotted; no ships were moving towards them, the pace or movement of ships hadn't increased since they entered the system. The Liberator hadn't yet been able to get a view of the Earth, but as that wasn't the goal it wasn't a priority and they carried on with the route to Mars. The route and tactic they were using made the trip very slow and tiresome, but that was a price worth paying to avoid any conflict.

Without any incidents- and evidently without detection- the Liberator arrived in orbit of the red planet. As they were now very close to an enemy stronghold, no time was wasted in heading down into the planet's atmosphere. 'I think we are good to move in, Captain.' Haver reported.

'Let's hope so, Baz.' the Captain navigated the ship down onto the planet. 'Let's see if Derrick's codes for the Hangar are still working.'

The ship descended through the atmosphere of the red, desolate planet and approached the old USSF base. The biospheres where people used to stay had been completely destroyed; all that remained was the outline of the structure's foundations, along with a great deal of rubble. Looking over the habitat was the shipyard and hangar. It was obvious that the structure had been massive; however, now all that remained was the remnants of the walls. There was no roof, or at least the roof was no longer on top of the structure; it was covering what would have been the floor of the hangar bay. Carrying on past the shipyard there was a large, suspiciously flat looking piece of land. Although it had obviously been excavated, it appeared as though there hadn't been any work started on the structure to be built there. As such, it had appeared to have been ignored during the Fedirian attack.

'That must be it.' announced SC, 'I'll bring us in just over the top, Baz you scan for an access signal.'

'Signal detected Captain, inputting our code now.' responded Haver.

The atmosphere was tense as the command crew waited for a response. 'I think that it's working, Captain.' reported Haver with relief.

Looking at the view screen, they could see the ground beneath them opening up, the two great slabs of rock disappearing sideways into the ground. The hole beneath the ship was easily large enough to absorb the Liberator, allowing the ship to descend beneath the surface. Carefully the mammoth vessel slipped underground, enlightening the ERF crew with a site that was a stark contrast to that above ground. No semblance of destruction; what was beneath, however, was a high tech landing pad with computers and displays all around. Large machinery attached to concrete walls showed what Derrick had described and he was right: this was more of a ship yard than a landing bay. However, the landing platform was large enough to comfortably house three Cruiser-sized vessels. Needless to say, the space was huge.

The Liberator touched down with a small bump, which wasn't a bad effort for SC's first attempt at landing such a large vessel. The hangar appeared deserted, but SC and his crew weren't convinced. 'Any life signs?' asked the Captain.

'Nothing that I can detect; however, there is such a strong dampening field in place down here that I would have trouble detecting us.' replied Haver.

'So we are confident that we have company down here, we just can't be sure how friendly it is,' offered Ward.

'Precisely,' responded SC. 'Commander Hill, ready your ground team; let's assume friendly but be prepared, so non-lethal force.'

'Yes Captain, I take it you will be joining us.' acknowledged the strike team leader.

'Myself, Haver and Ward will accompany you.' responded the Captain. 'Move out in five minutes.'

The ground team hit the floor of the hangar bay and immediately took up defensive positions. Although no other life forms had been detected or seen, they were unwilling to take any unnecessary risks. SC, Haver and Ward stuck beside Hill, who was leading the action. Taking their lead from him they followed the Commander alongside the hangar wall until a hatch was reached. Confident this was the best way into the facility, the remainder of the squadron positioned themselves in a semi-circle around the entrance. They quickly realised that the door was locked. Haver was sent in to bypass the locking mechanism and allow the team entry.

As Haver worked, SC took note of how quiet and eerie the Hangar was, especially as the doors which had opened to allow the Liberator to land had closed. There were working lights in the large space; however, they were not strong enough to adequately illuminate the whole bay, meaning that the available light left plenty of dark places to hide in, or potentially contained others who were already hiding.

Suddenly the hatch started to open, much to Haver's surprise. 'That wasn't me!'

'Quick, everybody, defensive positions.' called Hill.

Haver jumped away from the door whilst the team separated away from the semi-circle, leaving nobody in front if the hatch. The team lined up three meters away from the door on either side, preparing for any weapons fire.

Finally the hatch was fully open with everybody waiting. Nothing happened immediately, leading the tactical team to think it was Haver who had opened the door after all. Then it came, thundering weapons fire streaming out of the hatch, not hitting -or apparently aiming- at anything other than making sure the entrance was clear.

It became evident that this wasn't the actions of Fedirian soldiers, or even battle hardened human military: this was scared people trying to defend themselves against an unknown attacker. SC knew as well as anybody that unfortunately, there is nothing more dangerous than scared people with guns, so he began to speak, or shout would be more appropriate, 'Hold your fire! Hold your fire, we are friendly, we mean you no harm!'

Hill was looking at SC very strangely; his expression was trying to convey the message, 'What are you doing, they are shooting at us, they are the enemy.' However, that is quite a hard concept to put across eloquently with the use of only eyebrows and cheek muscles, so SC ignored the facial expressions and repeated his statement.

The firing stopped for about ten seconds, then it started again, then it stopped again after a few seconds. Ward, Hill and SC were now looking at each other confused, until a croaky voice was heard from inside the doorway, 'Who are you and what do you want?'

Continuing with the path he had started, SC responded, 'We are human, we are friendly and we need to use your facilities.'

Taking a chance, SC stepped out into the middle of the hatchway with his hands raised so that it was obvious he was unarmed. Slowly out of the darkness of the hatch a young looking man appeared. He wore overalls, not fatigues or a uniform, looking very much like a mechanic. He was armed and he kept his gun trained on SC as he approached. The landing team all raised their weapons at the approaching man, awaiting any sign that he might open fire.

It didn't take long for the mechanic to realise that he was face to face with a group of human soldiers, so carefully he lowered his weapon, keeping his eyes on SC the entire time. The Liberator's Captain signalled to his team to lower their guns and, for the first time since they landed, everyone took a moment to breathe.

Quickly yet carefully introductions were made; the mechanics name was Tony Sullivan, originally employed as the head shipbuilder on the Mars base before the attack. He had been working on a secret project in the underground shipyard when the assault began. As soon as shots were fired the evacuation procedure kicked in and people from the surface habitats started making their way to the underground bunker by means of quick escape tunnels. It had been discovered that the iron concentration in the ground made it impossible to scan through, so enemy ships who had destroyed the surface building would detect no sign of life underground.

After the attack Tony took control of the whole facility, as he was the most senior person, and started creating living quarters in a lot of the workshops and storage spaces for the eight hundred and twenty six people that they had in the facility. Food rationing was implemented, as although they appeared to have a three year supply, there was no guarantee that they would be able to supplement it at any point. SC listened with great interest to what had transpired and regaled Tony and his immediate compatriots of what had happened with the ERF over the past year. Tony confirmed that the base Scanners had detected the ERF fleet leaving the system one year ago; however, fear of being discovered prevented them from calling for help. Tony explained that he was unaware that there had been a colony set up on the Moon at the time due to the fact that the bases Scanners didn't reach far enough to detect them. However, a lot had changed within the past year.

Ward quickly brought up the subject of available medical equipment due to the rapidly deteriorating condition of Wilson. She was relieved to learn that the medical equipment needed to reverse the damage inflicted by the radiation was available in the base, so at SC's suggestion it was decided that they should return to the discussions of the current situation once they had gotten Wilson into the medical bay to allow the doctors to get to work. Tony agreed quickly and half of the landing team, lead by Ward along with 2 members of the Mars medical team, left to retrieve Wilson from the Liberator.

Whilst Wilson was being attended to, SC, Hill, Haver, Tony Hall and Amy Rover sat down in the makeshift Command Centre. Tony introduced Amy as his second in command and he thought she should take part in the meeting. Amy was in her early twenties, blonde, attractive, confident, and had a keen mind, which appeared to contain a good deal of deductive reasoning. She had been a military intelligence officer, junior grade, when the attack hit. All of her superiors had been off planet when the attack began and were either dead or somewhere else in the galaxy by this point, leaving her as the highest ranking intelligence officer in the system. SC explained that his fleet was in some need of repair without going into specifics; However, with luck it should be of a size capable of expelling the available fleet of Fedirian vessels, providing no more had arrived within the past year. But he really needed to know what the current situation was.

'Firstly,' Tony responded, 'there have been no new ships arriving to reinforce the Fedirian fleet, so assuming your count is correct, it should be the situation you are prepared for and we can check those numbers in a minute.' SC, Haver and Hill took on a look of relief when they heard the first news. 'However,' Tony continued, 'there might be a bigger problem if you don't act soon.'

'What do you mean?' Questioned the anxious Captain.

'They are building a space station and it looks like it's nearly complete,' replied the engineer, who was gesturing to the monitor. 'It looks like it will be a defensive platform, heavily armed and orbiting the Earth.'

SC and his team surveyed the view screen and there it was: a large hexagonal shaped space station. Although initially SC thought this to be a strange shape for the purpose, it started to make sense when he could see that each of the sides contained a launch pad for a Cruiser-sized vessel. Meaning that in an emergency, they could launch six large vessels at a time, giving an advantage over any conventional launch bay with the usual compliment of one large bay door.

From the size of the station it seemed to suggest that they could use the station as a dry dock for repairs for any size of craft. Closer investigation of the picture showed launch tubes for fighters, allowing the enemy to literally spray fighters out at any time in large numbers. Each corner contained a large cannon, which the sole purpose would be to obliterate anything that came near it. It was plain to see that if this station was fully functional, the ERF would have little or no chance of taking them out.

'Ok then,' stated SC matter-of-factly, 'best not hang about.'

Chapter 12

SC and his team, including Ward, who had now re-joined them, got too work assessing all the information given by Tony, whilst questioning Amy about her understanding of the enemy strength and fleet size. Both of them were more than happy to help. It seemed that they were enjoying the reality of not feeling abandoned on another planet with no hope. Having this influx of new people had them energised; it was also nice that they were able to share some of the vast amounts of information that they had been gathering for a year.

'We have tracked six large enemy vessels, two Cruisers and four destroyers. There are three small gunships, and we believe there are around one hundred fighters in space, either on patrol or docked with the ships or the new space station. That is complemented by around fifteen hundred more on the planet surface, alongside maybe a hundred and fifty small transport vessels. We estimate there are around fifty thousand troops on the ground. They have been building air defences but we think these are minimal at this point.' reported Amy.

'Wait a minute,' commanded a confused SC, 'what planet surface?'

'Earth,' responded the young intelligence officer.

'Earth was nuked, we were there. The entire planet's atmosphere was destroyed along with everything and everyone. The radiation will consume that planet for about ten thousand years. How can the Fedirians survive down there?' exclaimed a confused SC.

'Of course, you wouldn't know would you. I'm sorry; it seems that we missed something big.' Amy responded, 'Well, just after you left, we started expanding the range of our Scanners. We wanted to see if there was anyone else out there that we had missed. After about a month we were able to extend a communication signal far enough that it reached Earth. We started to transmit on an old intelligence channel, just to see if anyone was still alive; somebody picked up the transmission and replied. They helped us tap in to all of the remaining military sensors and satellites around the planet. With their help, we now have the ability to monitor the whole of the Earth, including the environmental conditions. We detected that the radiation in the atmosphere had returned to tolerable levels, and it is reducing day by day. We used our new found ability to examine the planet to bring up a topographical display, then after much examination we found that the Fedirian's have a large device that acts like a filter and is able to remove the radiated particles from the air and the soil and return them to normal. We don't know how it works, it's a little beyond our understanding, but I believe it works in a similar way to our medical devices that reduce the radiation in human cells. Their device is just on a much grander scale.' Amy finished her tale to be greeted by a room full of blank expressions and open mouths.

After what seemed like an eternity, in reality about a minute, Naomi was the first to recover. 'So you are saying that not only is the Earth a viable planet again, but that there are other people like us alive down there?'

Amy took a second and looked Naomi squarely in the eyes and with a small smirk and full conviction replied, 'Yes, that is exactly what I am saying.'

'Do we know how many?' Asked SC in shocked disbelief.

'Our best estimates has the human population on the planet at around two and a half million people, vastly spread out, mostly in the western hemisphere where there were a larger amount of fallout shelters.'

'Who is your contact on the ground?' Enquired the Acting Captain.

'Our initial contact was James Ironside, an American submarine Captain aboard a Los Angeles Class attack sub, but now we have a few contacts feeding us intelligence.'

'Two and a half Million people, and to think that I thought we were an endangered species.' replied SC.

'We will be,' replied Tony, 'if we don't do something soon.'

'What do you mean?' asked the young Captain.

'I think it is safe to assume that they didn't return the planet to normal and build a huge space station because they were planning on leaving anytime soon: there must be more to their plan than that. We need to know what it is and stop it if we are to survive as a species, because between you me and the gatepost, they look like they are moving in.' replied the engineer.

SC nodded in agreement, 'You're right; we have a plan to make.'

Using all the new information at their disposal, and including Tony and Amy in the discussions, the senior officers started to put down the basis for a plan. SC decided there needed to be a three way simultaneous attack, hitting the enemy on all sides at once, limiting the ability of the Fedirian's to call in support. SC figured that they had the resources to take out the Space Fleet, such as it was. However, if they drafted in the fifteen hundred fighters from the planet, then the tide would turn. Also whilst it was suspected that the space station wasn't fully operational, they had all watched Star Wars and nobody was willing to take that chance. So that meant an assault on the fleet was required, whilst simultaneously destroying the fighters on the ground and taking over the space station. Although this seemed like a lot, if SC could get his fleet into the system and have everything in place, it might just be doable.

Firstly they needed to plan the surface attack. Using the information supplied by Tony and Amy, it turned out that there were a number of manned military assets still in play on Earth; mostly submarines, six US, four Russian, two Japanese, two Israeli, one French, one Korean and one German. Unfortunately, they weren't yet able to make contact with any submarines aside from the Americans.

They would have to find another way to get in touch with the others in order to involve them. There were also other ground and air military assets, hidden in mountain locations where they were impossible to detect. The key to the success of this part, however, would be getting a small team to Earth to make contact with all the assets and co-ordinate them into an attack formation on the enemy bases.

'We need a how and where.' Stated Ward.

SC thought for a moment, and then leaned closer to the monitor, gesturing toward the Screen ahead. 'I'm not sure on the how yet, but looking at this map I am having an idea about the where. Amy, can you tell me if this ship here is what I think it is?'

Amy zoomed her image into where SC was pointing on the display. She selected the object and pulled up a Screen beside it, 'it's the HMS Edinburgh, a Royal Navy Destroyer, and the ship is unmanned but seems in one piece.'

'Why is she still afloat?' He asked to no-one in particular.

Amy turned to SC, 'It seems that Fedirian Scanners home in on life signs and destroy any targets. The only exception to that seems to be if something is presenting an immediate threat, you know, things such as drones. So probably because the ship was abandoned they never gave it a second look. Why?'

'If we could get there we have the facilities to transmit to all the military assets still active and formulate a battle plan.' responded the Captain.

Ward nodded in agreement, 'That's perfect, but how do we get there, without being detected? It will need a team and I think they would spot a squadron of Fire Starters long before we even got to Earth.'

'I might have something that could help with that.' stated Tony.

The group followed the engineer out into the hanger bay, heading over to the opposite side from where the Liberator was parked. The hangar bay lights came on and, no longer hidden under the cover of darkness, there was a dark grey coloured shuttle craft. 'This was one of the covert projects we were working on before the attack. We never got the chance to test it, but I am fairly confident it works.' offered Tony.

'What does it do?' Asked SC.

'It's a stealth shuttle; the panels are coated to deflect scans, creating an almost dead space if anyone was to look hard, with all life-signs being masked by a dampening field, similar to the one used in this facility. So it should be completely undetectable to the enemy.'

'I like it,' replied the Captain, 'I think we have our how, but now we have to figure out: who are we going to get to pilot it?'

'I'll do it, I'll lead the planet assault, if you'll allow it.' responded Ward.

'Are you sure?' asked SC.

'You need someone you can trust and the Edinburgh was my ship too, so it kind of makes sense.' stated Naomi.

The plan for the planet invasion was set: now they just needed to work out how to take out the space station. SC had other thoughts than taking it out, but first he needed some technical assistance. SC showed Tony the damage report of the Eagle, How long would it take for you to make it so that this ship could take a few hits and install the dampening field?'

'Realistically, I would want to tear it apart and start again, but at a push we would need a good week to fix this and install the field.' answered the engineer.

'What could you do if you had an hour?' Smiled the Captain slyly.

The Engineer held his hand to his head with a troubled look, 'Take a tour of it?' He joked. 'Not much to be honest; I could try and get the dampening field up but couldn't guarantee it would be up in an hour, and it's not really enough time to replace or repair any of the panels. Why, what do you have in mind?'

SC explained his plan to Tony and, although he had his doubts, he agreed to do what he could in the time he was given. They both decided that they would have to move quickly to ensure the best chance of success. But the sooner they could get their hands on the Eagle, the better.

SC would have to leave soon so he could return and collect the fleet. He elected to do this by flying Speedy back to rendezvous with the Swan, and catching a ride back to the fleet. He knew, however, that the moment the fleet turned up in the system, the fight would be on, and so every part would need to be ready to go straight away. As SC was set to leave for the Swan, Ward assembled her team for the flight to Earth. She was almost ready to go when she stopped Tony, 'Do you have a spare engineer that I can take with me? I'm not sure what state the Edinburgh's engines will be in when we get on-board.'

'I'm not sure who I have that would be familiar with those sorts of engines, to be honest; our people are trained in space ships, not Navy Destroyers.' replied Tony.

A voice came from across the room, 'Maybe I can help.'

Ward looked across and there was Wilson walking toward her with a massive smile on his face. 'Did you miss me?' He asked.

Naomi let her emotions get the better of her and ran to Geoff to embrace him. They held each other for a moment, Naomi whispering in his ear, 'I thought I had lost you.'

Geoff just cuddled her tightly before responding, 'You aren't ever getting rid of me.'

The embrace lasted for a few more seconds, and then both of them knew it was time to go to work. Almost instantly Naomi started filling him in on the plan. SC approached the pair and shook hands with the fleet's Chief Engineer, 'You did well saving that ship, and nobody would think any less of you if you chose to sit this one out.'

'Thanks, but there are jobs to be done, and I think I'm the only one around here who knows how to work the engines on that old tug that you used to sail on.' replied Geoff sarcastically.

Less of the old tug, she's a good ship.' replied the Captain. 'How is it that you know Royal Naval Destroyers?'

'I did some of my apprenticeship working on board the HMS Glasgow, back in 2005, just before she was decommissioned. Same type 42 destroyer. It was a shame they scrapped her in 2009; she would have been useful down there.' answered the engineer.

'Small world, the same fate would have befallen the Edinburgh if it hadn't been for budget cuts. She was re-commissioned in a hurry when the Navy found they couldn't afford the Type 45's, and it was no bad thing: that ship was built to take a pounding.' replied the Captain.

SC and Naomi gave each other a parting hug and wished the other luck as both set off for their respective craft; both with serious jobs to do and no guarantee of success or survival. Both were heavily reliant on the other; if either one failed to deliver what they required; the other was doomed to fail, also. But before any of the plan could happen, Ward needed to enter a heavily defended, enemy controlled world with an experimental ship and a crew of fifteen people, and SC just needed to slip out of the system undetected in a single man fighter and rendezvous with the Swan. It turned out that neither task would be particularly easy.

Ward and SC launched out of hidden launch tubes that ran below the surface of the red planet, these exited a few miles from the base. Their greatest advantage being that they reduced the risk of detection due to reopening the main hangar door. Once each craft was airborne they began flying in almost completely opposite directions. Ward decided a straight route would be best, cutting down the amount of time in open space. She kept her weapon system turned off so not to accidentally set off any alarms in the Fedirian patrol ships. The dampening field seemed to be working fine as they flew past the first enemy cruiser. She kept her distance but did not want to add too much time to the journey.

So far so good: the dampening field seemed to be blocking the life signs inside the shuttle, allowing them to consistently pass all the space ships in orbit around the planet. However, it was just as they entered the Earth's atmosphere that the problems began. The extreme heat caused by re-entry caused a spike in power usage to the shuttles' coolant system. This unfortunately cut power for a few seconds to the dampening field. This brief power outage was long enough to attract the attention of a passing air patrol that had been close to the re-entry point. It didn't take long for Ward to realise that there were enemy signals on an intercept course for them.

SC, on the other hand, had thought his job should be quite easy, as he could exit the system the same way that he came in, this time in a much smaller craft. That confidence was misplaced as he discounted the possibility of happenstance. Just as he was rounding Jupiter, he came head to head with a small patrol of three Fedirian fighters.

SC immediately opened fire on the enemy craft, causing damage to one of the three, before accelerating into a dive to avoid the slightly slower-to-react enemy ships. The damaged ship backed off immediately, leaving two fighters following the Fire Starter. Using a range of evasive manoeuvres, SC banked, rolled and dived; unfortunately, despite avoiding taking on damage, he could not get an attacking position on his pursuers. Trying a different approach, SC figured that Jupiter was a large planet, and he could give them the run-around around it for a while whilst he tried to evade them. The plan seemed to be working; SC was putting some distance between him and his pursuers and he was just getting ready to try a new tactic to get around and fire back on the attackers. Unfortunately, he had forgotten about the third craft, the one he had damaged just minutes before, which was now making its way toward SC in a pincer formation with the other two fighters.

Naomi was left with an altogether different problem: she had realised that the weapons systems on the shuttle was more than capable of defeating the incoming craft, however, if she allowed them to see her and report back, it would potentially make it impossible to covertly attack the enemy bases when the time came. She also couldn't risk leading the enemy craft to the Edinburgh, otherwise they could destroy the very thing they needed to do the job that they were there to do.

'How far out are they?' Asked Geoff.

'They'll be able to see us in about ninety seconds.' replied Naomi.

'What options do we have?'

'Stand and fight, or hide.' she responded.

'Where can we hide? There is nothing around for miles.' Geoff answered quickly.

'Tell everyone to hold their breath.' replied the pilot.

Without slowing down, the shuttle took a course which drove them straight into the ocean, the water enveloping the ship within seconds. The waves that were created took a while to die down; however, those waves were all that the passing enemy patrol saw, a massive splash in the Atlantic Ocean. Their scans revealed nothing abnormal: no life signs and no weapons. deciding the original contact must have been a glitch, the enemy craft carried on with their patrol.

SC had no idea he was heading into a trap until it was too late. The ship ahead of him was firing before he even saw it. Despite manoeuvring quickly to avoid the majority of the incoming fire, he took on some damage to his wing, cutting down on his ability to turn fast. The ships closing from behind started to fire along with the one in front. SC started to fire ahead of him, figuring that if he was going to die he was going to try and take at least one of the enemy craft with him. His shots made contact with the lone ship and caused it to explode in a ball of fire. As he awaited the same situation to befall him, he turned his fighter to face the enemy and a second ball of fire ignited in the dark sky, this time from the chasing craft. The last remaining fighter was caught off guard and distracted by the loss of his partner and he hadn't realised that SC had completed his turn and was now directly in his sights. Shots came from both sides, destroying the target in little time. SC looked around to see the identity of his saviour, when he heard the voice of Sally Karran, 'Never leave your wingman!'

Chapter 13

SC and Sally were arguing when they arrived on the Scanner of the Swan. Selina tuned in to the Fire Starters' communications frequency to hear SC's raised voice, 'I have already said thank you for your help, but you weren't supposed to be out there.'

'I am your wingman, and I have been for months, we have each other's back, that's how we stay alive. I understand you like to go off playing the Lone Ranger, but you cannot do it all on your own; next time you go somewhere, take me with you, you need someone to have your back.' protested the young pilot.

'I agree with Sally, the girl has a point,' Selina chimed in, 'By the way, you might want to keep radio chatter down to a minimum in enemy space.'

'Yeah, yeah, yeah, I feel ganged up on. I am sorry I won't go off and leave you again. In the future you can come on all my suicide missions.' replied SC with sarcasm in his voice.

'Good.' smirked Karran.

'Now Selina, would you please stop nosing into our conversation and do something useful, like opening the hangar doors?' requested SC. Five seconds later the hangar doors of the Swan opened and the two pilots landed their crafts inside.

A little worse for wear but still in one piece, the stealth shuttle rose out of the ocean under its own power, the defensive shield flickering badly. 'How did you know that would work?' Inquired Wilson looking astonished.

'I didn't, just kind of hoped it would.' replied a smirking Naomi.

Geoff just shook his head and laughed, 'Did we take on any damage?'

Ward looked around at the different consoles; there weren't any flashing lights that didn't belong there, so she responded, 'It doesn't appear so, however, I would probably want it looked at before breaking atmosphere in it again.' Quickly the course was set to lead the shuttle back to its original heading, the HMS Edinburgh.

Once aboard the Swan, SC requested that Selina get the ship on its way to the fleet and he would explain what had transpired on Mars whilst they were moving. Within seconds of the order being given the Swan took off at full overdrive to head back to the fleet. SC explained to Selina about the state of the planet, the enemy numbers, the space station and what the plan was. When he finished he turned to see his formers Captain's face in disbelief, visibly shocked that her home still existed, that her species wasn't as ragtag and small as she had thought, as they all had assumed. With a small tear in her eye she asked, 'Do you really think we can take it back?'

SC looked at her thoughtfully, looking straight into her eyes he said softly, 'If we don't do it now, it's possible we never will.'

Bothered by the lack of response to her actual question, Selina asked again, 'But do you think we can?'

'I hope so,' he answered, looking solemn, 'I really hope so.'

The stealth shuttle neared the coordinates. Looking out of the reinforced window, there was a beautiful sight to see, the HMS Edinburgh, in all her glory, still afloat and looking completely identical to how she had looked when they abandoned her seventeen months ago. Naomi thought it was amazing that the Destroyer had been left alone; however, it did make sense, as an unmanned ship wasn't a threat. What would be the point of destroying it? It took some skilful piloting to negotiate the landing of the shuttle on the small helicopter pad at the rear of the ship, but the skilled pilot managed it.

As soon as they landed the crew quickly disembarked, with everyone heading to assigned stations. The crew had been given instructions on what their roles were to be; normally, a ship such as this would require a substantially larger crew than eighteen people. Unfortunately though, this was all they had. Geoff along with a few others headed straight to the engine room, as getting the ship operational was the most important part of the mission: the Edinburgh needed to be able to move, but also fight, and they needed to be quick as there was no telling when another patrol may pass. Naomi, along with three others, headed to the bridge of the ship. They needed to start making contact with the other human naval factions to build up a picture of whether or not they would be willing to help so she could formulate an attack plan. In the meantime, there was a small crew checking ordinance and ensuring the ships' weapon systems were functioning in the event of enemy detection. Before long the ship was up and running like it had never been abandoned: all weapons systems were locked and loaded and Ward had made contact with Ironside and was in the process of contacting the foreign submarines.

Wilson made his way to the bridge, enjoying the culture shock of being back outside, the wind hitting his face, breathing actual air. After a year and a half in space he had begun to think that he would never breathe real air again, or stand in the open, allowing the sun to run over him. The feeling was amazing and he knew that they had no choice but to be successful, as he desperately wanted to come home for good.

The engineer reached the bridge as Naomi was finishing a call with a Russian submarine captain. Wilson stood and waited until she was finished, 'Yes!' Ward shouted as she put the receiver down.

'Good news, I take it.' stated the engineer.

'They are all in, all the active submarines that we know about are eager to get involved. It would seem they have spent a long time waiting to make a move, but knew the likelihood of a solo attack would end in assured destruction. Being part of a co-operative attack gives them confidence of causing maximum destruction; even if the assault is not successful they will have dealt a great deal of damage, and these are Naval people, they want to do their bit.' replied the new ship Captain.

'Excellent news. You'll also be happy to know that the ship is all ready to go: engines are turning over great, weapons systems are working perfectly, but we have them powered down for now so not to attract any unwanted attention.' replied Wilson.

'Good, it seems we are just about ready to go then, we just have to try to move into our attack position, without being noticed.' Naomi stopped to think for a moment. 'I wonder how SC is getting on.'

The experience SC had had was much the same as Ward's. He easily convinced the other Captains that the chance of returning home was too good to miss. SC was able to achieve quick approval of his plan. There were concerns that it was a little risky, but all together as a group they had come to trust the former Navy Pilot. It was obvious that he had done as much as possible to limit the danger, despite the plans' heavy reliance on a lot of things going right.

All the Captains returned to their ships to prepare for the coming battle and ready their crews for the chance to go home. The time schedule agreed between Ward and SC meant that the fleet didn't have to leave straight away, but that the ships should be prepped and ready to go at the allotted time. SC knew that in order for this plan to work, the timing would have to be bang on without space for compromise. They were having to coordinate a three pronged attack over a galaxy, throughout a solar system, on a planet through land, air and sea; this would be no ordinary assault. Although nothing had been ordinary for a long time now, this was hitting a new level. Nobody in the known universe had ever planned such a campaign.

With all sides prepared there was little left to do other than wait, a concept that did not sit well with SC, Ward, or, as it would appear, a certain North Korean Sub Captain.

Captain Lee was in command of the last remaining Whiskey Class Submarine in the world. Before that, however, it was the last remaining one in the Republic of Korea Navy. The Whiskey class was an old soviet submarine, of which the Republic of Korea had had four. However in recent years, they had been decommissioned and dismantled, all apart from one.

During the attack on Earth, Captain Lee had kept his crew alive and ship intact, not by clever tactics and shrewd use of strategy, but by hiding. Although it might be said that when facing an opponent of far superior offensive capabilities that hiding may in fact be the best strategy, the truth was Lee didn't realise the fight was going on. Just prior to the attack on Earth, Captain Lee had reached the decision to defect from the Republic and flee with his ship and crew to the US. However, in order to pull off such a feat, he would have to fake the destruction of the Submarine, lay low, and then discreetly make his way to US waters.

He had already faked an explosion which would make it seem as though the ship had experienced a catastrophic failure, causing it to meet its end. Once that was complete, the Captain directed the sub to head into deep waters in order to hide whilst other Republic vessels investigated the explosion. Keeping complete radio silence, Lee and his crew went dark for three days. After evidently no detection, he set about making sail for the US. Not wanting to attract unwanted attention, he kept the submarine deep and away from periscope depth, hindering his ability to see what was happening to the outside world. Once approaching US controlled waters, and not wanting to cause an international incident or, in fact, be destroyed by trigger happy Americans, he brought the Submarine up in order to send an encoded message to the US military. It was then he started to realise that things weren't as they should be. Although tempted by the opportunity to launch his cruise missiles at the alien invaders, it was apparent that a single attack such as this would do little to resolve the overall issue, so he made the decision to hide again until a better opportunity presented itself.

Having been contacted by this "Ward" character, it would seem that the better opportunity had arrived. There was a plan to fight back, and Lee wasn't about to miss out on it. However, the submarine Captain thought he had noticed a flaw with Naomi's plan. Using his knowledge of the situation, he surmised that there was one enemy base that would be left unscathed. He had suggested to Ward about his ship taking out that one, then moving on to the target she had given; however, she had replied that she would be taking that one out with a Destroyer. It didn't seem likely that Ward would be able to sail a destroyer close enough to the target to destroy it, as this was the advantage of using submarines, so that they wouldn't attract any attention from the enemy as they got into position. Lee decided as both targets were close together he would hit Ward's base first then head to his own.

This would prove to be a mistake.

Chapter 14

The time had arrived: all four of the well-functioning ships of the ERF formed a defensive line at the entrance to the Sol System, more than forty Fire Starters lined up with them. All positioned and readied to maximum battle-stations, with the Dreadnought positioned a safe distance back from the fleet, enabling it to use its long guns to assist in the attack, but keep out of the firing range of enemy vessels. Although work had been carried out on the flagship, it was still very vulnerable. The arrival position was not to bring forth the entire force of the Fedirian defences, but to attract the interest of the roaming patrol ships.

Prior to the arrival of the fleet, the Eagle had arrived in the system, discreetly making its way towards the facility on Mars, knowing, that the chances of sneaking the Eagle, in its fragile state, into the subterranean base without detection was unlikely. Now on the outer edge of the system, the Fedirian patrols had something else to pay attention too. This made the final stretch of the journey remarkably easier, with the Eagle descending straight into the red planet and landing within minutes.

Tony was rather upset to see that SC hadn't been exaggerating about the battered condition of the craft he had to deal with. True to his word, the ship-builder had his team start work without a moments delay. Amy approached SC as soon as he appeared. 'I've had word from Ward that everything is in place on her side.'

'Excellent,' he responded, 'within the next forty minutes she can start her assault. Are you ready for your part in this?'

'I hope so.' replied the nervous looking intelligence officer.

The Fedirian scout ships had reported back to base that they had detected some movement at the outer rim of the system and would be checking it out. However, communications would become difficult from there, so a backup ship may need to be dispatched to relay messages. The Fedirian scout party was made up of a Destroyer-type craft along with a small gunship and five fighters. Quickly but carefully, they made their way to the coordinates of the movement.

By the time the scout party had realised what it had encountered it was too late, all five ERF ships opened fire upon the Destroyer with the Fire Starters surrounding the support vessels. Within seconds the fight was over, and the scout party was eliminated without casualty to the ERF. Now for stage two of the plan.

The attack force on the planet was moving into final positions and the Edinburgh was discreetly rounding the Florida Keys. Thanks to Geoff extending the stealth shield from the shuttle around the Type 42 Destroyer, they had so far been undetected. This was when Naomi realised things weren't the way they should be. 'Sonar is picking up a submarine very close to our position, Commander.' reported the new communications chief on board the Edinburgh.

'Did we miss one?' Asked Ward, 'Is this a submarine we didn't account for? Get in touch with Amy on Mars, she needs to check the transponders and see who that is.'

The Fedirian backup destroyer that had come out to act as a message relay could pick up no sign of the scout party, they reported back to the fleet. Command advised caution and would send a backup vessel to support them in the search. If nothing showed up soon a full scale search would be initiated with a considerable force. In the meantime, all ERF vessels were hidden grouped closely to Uranus, making them virtually undetectable for the moment. Unless an enemy craft were to fly right past them.

As Tony and his crew raced through their modifications to the Eagle, installing a dampening field, patching holes and installing an additional power generator for the shields, Amy was checking the transponder signals from all detectable vessel, 'It's Lee,' Amy barked through the comm unit, 'Lee is out of position.'

'Thank you Amy, I'd better find out what he is doing as we have only a few minutes until we launch.' replied Ward.

Just as Naomi picked up the transmitter to contact Lee, she saw the Whiskey class submarine surface. Whilst still confused to his intention, his missile doors started to open, seconds later two cruise missiles fired out of the top of the sub. Ward was in disbelief as the submarine subsequently dived and started moving away fast and noisy. Two brilliant explosions were seen in the distance, obviously from the impact of the missiles finding their target. But the ERF had just lost the one thing they needed the most: the element of a synchronised, surprise attack.

Unfortunately that wasn't the only problem to occur: after the disappearance of the scout patrol, the Fedirian's had moved to high alert and had detected the radio transmission from Earth to Mars. A Fedirian Cruiser had already been dispatched to investigate the Red Planet before the explosions occurred on Earth. Arriving on Mars at the rough location of the signal, the responding Cruiser opened fire on the remnants of the USSF base, hoping to discover and destroy the source of the transmission. Unfortunately, due to the fact that the secret hangar door had been opened twice recently it had cleared away some of the natural camouflage that had been previously utilised, making it obvious that something wasn't quite right. It didn't take long for the Cruiser to realise the source of the transmission and changed its pattern of fire to concentrate specifically on the covered door. Needless to say that none of this was part of the well thought out plan.

Ward ordered every vessel to launch their missiles. Although slightly ahead of schedule, they needed to make the most of the surprise that they had left. The Edinburgh, along with Lee, made tracks toward the second target zone nearby. Unfortunately, due to the prior warning of the early attack, the fleet of fighters at the second base had already taken off. One hundred and fifty enemy craft were now airborne and looking for someone to shoot at.

The only good news was that all the other vessels had been successful in destroying their targets completely, allowing the recently re-commissioned ground forces to move in from hiding and converge on the coordinated attack points and start taking back control of territories long since surrendered. It was well known that this would be a short lived success if the Fedirian space fleet, weapons platform, and now the one hundred and fifty fighters looking for something to destroy, weren't dealt with quickly.

The Mars underground base hangar door could only take so much abuse and it was reaching its limit. Suddenly, the door began to open. Unsure of what was happening, the Fedirian Cruiser stopped firing as they wanted to see what it was that they were shooting at. The Fedirian ship waited for over a minute, and although their sensors could pick up movement beneath the surface, no ship had become apparent. Just as they were about to begin firing again, they detected a ship rising out of the Hangar. Finally, they were about to get the first look at their target, but before the Fedirian ship got its first look, the new vessel opened fire on the Cruiser. The immediate and devastating damage that was delivered made it obvious that the enemy was not expecting the firepower of the Liberator to be attacking it back. Never had they encountered something so powerful. This unexpected ship seemed to have strong defensive shields and no obvious weakness. Very soon it was apparent that the Fedirian Cruiser was outgunned and was calling out for help. The Mars base closed their Hangar door and went back into hiding, whilst the Liberator made short work of the Cruiser.

Now that surprise was out of the way, Ward had little choice but to take control of the stealth shuttle again and take to the sky whilst simultaneously Wilson took charge of the Edinburgh, aiming all sea to air weaponry at the enemy craft and engaging them. It was pretty obvious that they were massively outgunned and would not last long with one aircraft and one ship fighting the battle against one hundred and fifty opponents. The defensive shields on the stealth shuttle were holding up well, as Ward found herself the subject of target lock from three ships as she was pursuing one, the Edinburgh's anti-aircraft gun was whirring so fast it had nearly deafened those few crew who were available to operate it. But without a change of circumstances the attacking fighters would soon be victorious.

Seconds later Naomi's luck changed, 'Lots of contacts coming in,' yelled Geoff through the comm unit, 'and they are friendly!'

A moment later the sky was filled with all manner of fighter jets, including Harrier Jump-jets, Eurofighters, and F/A 18 Hornets, to name but a few. It was eventually counted that there was around fifty of these jets in the air, fully armed and ready to fight. Although still outnumbered, Ward and her team had a controllable situation, and suddenly these one hundred and fifty opponents, whose numbers were now decreasing, were now a beatable entity.

Having defeated the initial Cruiser, the Liberator broke free of Mars orbit before encountering a less than friendly Fedirian welcome party, including one Cruiser, two destroyers and one gunship accompanied by around eighty fighter craft. All parties opened fire at once, and although the Liberator was well defended, it was not equipped to handle an assault of this magnitude single handed. Luckily for the crew of the advanced ship they didn't have to. Moments later saw the arrival of the Swan, the O'Neil, the Alexandra and the Valiant, along with around forty Fire Starters.

The Liberator and the Valiant combined firepower to attack the Cruiser, leaving the O'Neil and the Alexandra to engage each of the Destroyers and the Swan concentrated its attack upon the gunship, leaving forty Fire Starters to tangle with eighty enemy Fighters. This was a fairly evenly matched contest, stacked slightly in favour to the ERF due to the Liberators' massive firepower. However, the race was on to disable these vessels as soon as possible, as there was another destroyer and gunship still out there, which if it were to join the battle may turn the tide. The Dreadnought was staying hidden as it could not realistically withstand any assault, and with the exception of it long guns would not be much help to the ERF.

The Swans entanglement with the smaller gunship was not easy, as although the enemy was smaller and less powerful, it was also harder to hit. This, combined with the fact that the Swan was unable to use its normal tactic of avoidance due to it normally being the smaller craft, it was having quite a battle. The O'Neil was easily a match for the destroyer it was against, throwing a lot of firepower forward and using its manoeuvrability to avoid taking on damage, meaning it had the upper hand on its opponent.

The Alexandra lacked the movement of the O'Neil and the Swan and was left trading head to head blows with the enemy craft. Realistically, to ensure victory, it required a little assistance. Assistance it was sure to get any moment as the Valiant and the Liberator were making short work of the Cruiser. Luckily for the Valiant, the enemy was laying the majority of its firepower into the Liberator, which was more than happily giving it back. Before long the Liberator dealt the final blows to the enemy Cruiser, causing it to explode in a huge ball of fire and freeing up the two ERF vessels to assist in the remaining fights.

The fleet of Fire Starters had their work cut out for them, taking on double the odds, but were just managing to hold their own. After the destruction of the enemy Cruiser, the Liberator threw them a bone and used pinpoint weaponry to take out fifteen of the smaller crafts in a matter of seconds, throwing the enemy fighter group into disarray and making it easier for the Fire Starters to try mopping up the rest.

Down on the planet Ward started to feel that they had gotten over the worst of the fight, and although there still seemed to be around fifty of the enemy crafts left, that number had become much more manageable than what they had been dealing with. Suddenly something had changed, and the remaining enemy fighters broke off their attack against the Earth fighters and changed course, heading straight to outer space and leaving Naomi with a dilemma as she had the only Earth based ship that could follow them up. Realistically, she knew that one ship versus fifty had no chance, and there was also the fact she wasn't convinced her ship wouldn't blow up whilst breaking orbit, but she also knew she had to try, as she couldn't just have fifty fighters join the space attack, not knowing what the situation with that was. She set her pursuit course and followed the enemy into space.

Making it through the atmosphere was just part one of her worries, as it turned out the little stealth shuttle was better put together than she gave it credit for. As it made it back into space with no problem at all, the second worry was she was catching up with the enemy fighters. Locking weapons on the closest one, she began to fire, direct hit, that was one down; unfortunately she had just acquired the attention of all the remaining fighters. Turning around, they decided to destroy this one ship before resuming course. They began to target the stealth shuttle. Naomi was preparing for what was sure to be a very short fight when she witnessed six explosions from the back of the pack, then another six. Her forty nine attackers had, within a few seconds, just been reduced to thirty seven. The enemy suddenly lost interest in Naomi and began turning around, bang another six explosions. Not being one to look a gift horse in the mouth, she began to open fire on her much numerically superior enemy.

Ward still couldn't see where her help had come from, only the continuous explosions in the dark sky, until a voice came through her comm unit, 'Thought you could use the help, Commander. Give us a minute and we will help you finish these off.' That cool clear voice belonged to Sally Karran: it was her and the rest of the Dark Knights who were making short work of the enemy fighters. It seemed that as the Liberator was taking off from the landing bay on Mars, the little squadron of Fire Starters launched out of the hidden tubes that Naomi had used herself, and here they were, just in the nick of time to ensure that no additional enemy crafts joined the space battle.

The only additional ships to join the battle were the Destroyer, gunship and around ten fighters that had been on patrol. Unfortunately for the patrol, they encountered the battle just as the O'Neill was delivering the final blow to the last enemy destroyer, leaving five battle ready ERF ships to dispose of the remaining Fedirian attackers. That engagement would not take long, so much so that the Dreadnought did not mind coming out of hiding before the battle was complete. The sense of relief was short lived as Haven shouted through the comm system, 'Swan, bank left now!'

The pilot of the Swan was quick to react; However, they still took on damage from the long stream of plasma fire that had emerged from the station. Riley announced from the O'Neil, 'I suggest we move out of the range of that weapon quickly, before someone is toast.'

The suggestion had barely come over the comm unit when a second blast came out, hitting the Valiant, square on. Luckily, the ship hadn't taken much damage up until that point, so it was able to withstand the blast, but agreed it could not take another. This led all ERF vessels to set a speedy course behind Mars and away from immediate danger. 'What's going on?' Shouted Clarke, 'I thought that station wasn't operational?'

Haver responded, 'It's not supposed to be, sir, but it's obviously further ahead than we had thought.'

'Lieutenant, where is your Captain? I assumed SC was in charge over there?' Demanded Clarke.

'No, sir, he isn't.' replied the young officer.

'Then who is in charge? And where is SC?'

'Sorry, Sir, I am currently in command of the ship,' replied Haver, 'the Captain is aboard the space station.'

Chapter 15

When the Fedirian Cruiser started its assault on the Mars base, and the hangar doors began to open, the enemy Cruiser stopped firing, the Eagle-with its new dampening field in place- ascended quickly out of the hangar, leaving the scene behind undetected whilst the Liberator followed it out and engaged the enemy. Whilst all attention was focused on the space battle, the damaged but barely – visible-to-sensors Eagle set course for the space station, containing a small crew including SC, Hill, Rover and Hill's Marines, along with Derek Strong and his crew in command of the ship, using their practical invisibility to manoeuvre the Eagle to the topside of the station and dock with it. The hope had been that whilst the other battles raged on, that they would be able to take the space station by surprise and capture it before anyone was the wiser. Unfortunately, that didn't seem to have happened yet.

The ERF fleet found themselves unable to communicate with the Eagle or the landing party, inviting the need for a new plan that involved destroying the Space station, as that alone seemed to be the only barrier to total victory. The real challenge would be how to get close enough to the station without being hit. Judging by the firepower they had witnessed, any assault would likely lead to mass casualties on the human side, without any real assurance of victory. Haver and Laverty pleaded with the other Captains to give SC some time; he hadn't let them down yet and there was no reason to assume that he would now.

Meanwhile, on board the space station....

'Hill, can you see another way around?' Shouted SC as he was ducking plasma shots that were whizzing past his head.

Hill surveyed the chaos and carnage that they were absorbed in. 'Not really, we have forces all around us.' he responded, 'Looks like this is the only way to the Command Centre from here. If we can't break through soon, we will have to try and retreat to the Eagle; staying here will just get us killed.' In front of the ERF landing party was a mixture of automated defences and Fedirian soldiers, intent on defending their stronghold and most valuable weapon.

SC and his team had hoped this task would be easier, as mostly everything had seemed to go to plan up until now: the surprise attack should have been a sure -fire winner. After leaving Mars and making their way undetected to the Space station, it appeared that they had managed to dock without setting off any alarms. Based on an extrapolated layout, they had estimated that the Command Centre would be only around three hundred meters from the docking point, along what appeared to be a reasonably straight corridor. There were a couple of other routes visible, but all appeared to be longer ways around and that added time and complication. So with a straight route and the element of surprise, a three hundred metre stretch seemed to be a workable solution which would accomplish the mission easily within the time limits set.

The reality was that it wasn't as big a surprise as they had hoped for, as the Fedirians detected the ship pretty much as soon as it had docked; However, rather than sounding the alarm, they discreetly moved troops into position and turned on all automated defence systems, so that as soon as the humans entered the passage way from the ship they would be ambushed. Two marines were killed as soon as the trap was sprung, causing the rest of the team to dig in to the sides for cover. Weapons fire was coming from the front and the back, meaning the landing party had no option of escape. The strike team could have attempted a return to the Eagle, but the Fedirian's employed an electronic lockdown of the hatch as soon as the ERF troops were in the station. Amy had managed to get access to a door panel and from there she was able to close and seal the blast door behind them, cutting off the assault from one side and just leaving the enemy ahead to deal with. The ERF had made some slow progress along the corridor, covering around thirty metres before their advance had been stopped due to the ferociousness of the automated blasters. Now they were stuck in a stalemate with no hopes of forward progression, and this time they didn't have someone in the control room to help them out. They needed a solution, and fast.

Amy Rover was living up to her title as an intelligence officer as she had been studying the station plans for an alternative. 'Captain, I think I might have found something.' she declared, much to SC's relief.

SC worked his way closer to her, carefully avoiding sporadic fire. Once he reached the intelligence officer he asked 'What do you have?'

Amy pointed at the ceiling of the passageway as she started to explain, 'It would seem that there is a very small maintenance area just above the corridor that we might be able to use; someone could crawl along it to get behind the enemy and throw a grenade down behind them. It may also be possible to deactivate the automated guns from there.'

SC reviewed the Schematics. 'OK, I like it, but that looks pretty small, how many people do you think we can get in there?'

Amy looked back at him with a look of disappointment on her face and explained, 'It's not like the USSF ones, it wasn't designed as a crawl space for engineers; more as an open and operate panel. However, I believe I may just be able to fit. But we would need to make sure they don't see me going up, or it will be game over.'

SC looked back at her concerned, 'This part of it I don't like so much. Are you sure about this, because if you do it I can't protect you. I also can't be sure that if you throw the grenade that the explosion won't kill you.'

'I don't need protecting, and it's all we have, sir; also, I'm pretty sure the bulkhead will protect me from the blast.' answered the brave young intelligence officer.

'OK then, let's do it.' commanded SC. He wasn't happy, but conflict called for quick decisions. Amy pointed out the access panel behind them; now all they needed was the distraction. SC called for Pillar to come back and help him, as they would need to get Amy into the shaft quickly. He handed her a grenade and ensured she had her sidearm. Hill was directed to start popping smoke grenades down the corridor, as many as he could, and follow it up with massive suppression fire.

As soon as the Hill started his attack, SC, Pillar and Amy stepped out into the middle of the gang way, hoisting the slim young officer up to the roof. Due to the amount of ERF firepower coming through the smoke, there was very little enemy firepower coming back, and certainly nothing accurate, as visibility had been completely cut off. Within a few seconds Amy was in position in what could only be described as a remarkably tight space, which she could barely move herself through. But move she did, knowing she would need to crawl her way forward around fifty metres to get behind the line of Fedirian troops. Slowly and silently Amy made her progress. In the meantime, the troops on the ground kept up their attack, not wanting it to seem as though there was something else going on. Anxiety started to spread through the force in the conflict, and it seemed to take an eternity for the young officer to reach her destination. In reality, due to the tightness and difficulty of movement, it probably took her around ten minutes, but for those exchanging fire, ten minutes felt like a life time.

Once in position, Amy opened the hatch behind the line of Fedirian troops. Taking the opportunity, she looked around, seeing nothing but a closed blast door behind them. Carefully, the young intelligence officer took her aim and threw the grenade into the pack of enemy soldiers, ending the deadlock. The explosion was powerful enough to kill all enemy troops in the passageway and caused some damage to the automated gun; although it was still firing, it had dropped to half power, which allowed the ERF team to breathe a small sigh of relief. Amy worked her way back along the tight service space so that she was directly above the weapon. There was a service hatch directly above it, which allowed her to reach down and deactivate the device at the source. The standoff in the tunnel had ended for the moment, SC and Pillar helped retrieve Amy from the crawl space, and together with the rest of the team, they regrouped to discuss how they would move forward.

'Can you open the blast door?' SC asked Amy.

'I believe so,' responded the young officer, 'it's not too difficult a system to get 'round, which is why I am slightly confused as to why the Fedirian's haven't opened the one behind us. I closed it as a temporary measure to buy us some time, but they should have been able to bypass it the same way as I will attempt to do on that one ahead of us.'

SC considered her comments, 'What do think had happened?'

'I think they have pulled all troops back to the Command Centre; I think behind the door ahead of us is two hundred metres filled with Fedirian soldiers as a last line of defence.' replied Amy. 'Behind us I believe is an empty corridor.'

SC thought for a moment; he was presented with two scenarios: the path in front was shorter, but potentially contained countless troops between his team and their goal; and the path behind, which was longer, but with potentially less threats. Well, at least until the Fedirians worked out what the invaders were doing.

'I think I have a plan.' announced the Captain.

SC contacted the Eagle and told them to prepare to detach, although they would need to stay within the inside of the station circumference, otherwise they would become a target for the stations' powerful guns, Derek understood and didn't question the request. Amy was asked to open the rear blast door, whilst the Marines stood ready. Just as the young officer had suspected, the door opened and there was no welcoming party. So far so good; the majority of the ERF troops filed out into the rear corridor to ensure they secured that position. The young intelligence officers next job was to prepare the forward blast door to open, but with a time delayed release. In the meantime, Hill and Pillar rigged up explosives all around the blast door and along the bulkhead wall, which was also the outside hull. Within ten minutes everything was set and all parties were prepared to go.

Hill looked at SC and asked, 'Do you think this will work?'

'As long as your explosives do their job, then I think we have a good shot. Amy, how much time do I have on that door?' Inquired the Captain.

'Fifteen seconds after you press it, the door will open,' she responded.

'You do realise, I am not Usain Bolt, don't you? Fifteen seconds to run one hundred meters isn't long.' he replied.

Amy let out a chuckle, 'Best I can do, I'm afraid.'

SC looked at them all and smiled. 'Let's do it then.'

Amy, Hill, Pillar and the rest of the team retreated back to the rear blast door. Scouts had been sent along the corridor to the next door, which was open to ensure that the team would have a clear exit. SC stood at the forward blast door and gave the order for Derek to detach; as soon as the former Flight Commander felt the movement of the detaching ship, he hit the switch for the door timer, which was also connected to the explosives timer. As soon as he hit the switch SC started running as fast as he could to the rear blast door, which he found, with the weight of all the tactical gear he was wearing, was no easy thing. He reached the other door just as the forward door began to open; quickly Hill closed the door just as the explosives went off.

It was a violent bang that shook the entire station; the power of the explosives killed the first few enemy soldiers instantly. However, the corridor full of Fedirians was relatively safe for around two seconds, until the outer hull of the space station gave out and sucked all the occupants of the metal tube into space.

There was no time to waste now for the ERF troops: they had the diversion they needed, with the added bonus that a large group of enemy troops had just met an untimely end. However, there was no way of knowing how many troops were still on board or how many of them stood between the assault team and the Command Centre. The Eagle detaching at the same time was designed to make it seem as though the ERF troops had left and abandoned the invasion; it also helped ensure that the already vulnerable ship didn't take any damage from the explosion. However, now Derek had the more difficult task of keeping the ship away from the powerful space station guns whilst traversing its way to the other side of the station to re-dock. This part of the plan was imperative, as it would mean any remaining troops would be sent to defend that side of the station whilst the real attack group made their way on the opposite side from the Eagle, albeit the long way round.

The explosion from the space station did not go unnoticed by the ERF fleet who were watching from afar. After seeing the difficulty that the Eagle was having, Ward, along with her team of Fire Starters, rushed from their forward position and opened fire on the station, attracting the attention of the gun platforms who were hopelessly trying to hit the very small targets with very large guns. Once the Eagle reached its position, Ward's team pulled out, taking care to avoid incoming shots when they went. Soon the Dark Knights were outside of the range of the space stations vicious weaponry.

Not for the first time today, SC's plan had worked like a charm, with the ERF team encountering no resistance this time on their route to the Command Centre; with the exception of one last blast door which Amy took no time at all to open. Unfortunately, the last blast door led straight into the Command Centre which was being held by a dozen heavily armed Fedirian soldiers who were determined not to lose control of their fleet's most dangerous weapon, and their only hope of surviving the conflict.

As soon as the door opened Hill was immediately hit by a shot from an enemy weapon, causing him to drop to the ground where he was quickly joined by his team, who had hit the floor in defence. It took a moment before SC realised that the Commander wasn't moving. With shots still whizzing overhead, SC pulled his friend back from the door. One look at his face and it was obvious that he had been killed instantly. Pushing aside an overwhelming need to grieve, SC realised that there really wasn't time, and now he had to take command of this attack and finish what had been started.

'Pillar, get over here!' shouted the Captain. Pillar traversed his way to his superior's position, taking note of his dead Commander's body as he reached him.

'Oh my god, is he dead?' asked the young second officer.

'Unfortunately yes, but there will be a whole lot more of us sharing his fate if we don't do something quickly.' answered SC.

Pillar nodded his head in agreement. Feeling a tear forming in his eye before summoning it to go back up, 'OK Sir, what do you think we should do?'

'Do you have any grenades?'

The young soldier considered his request momentarily before replying; 'Only smokers, we used all the live ones when we were pinned down in the other corridor.'

Time was running out and the newly promoted Captain knew it, fully aware that they couldn't hold the position indefinitely and knowing that they would likely be picked off or surrounded if they waited long enough. 'We need to split their fire and gain a better position to fire back, as they seem to have all the cover in there.'

'Ok I agree, so what are you thinking?'

SC smirked at the marines' new commanding officer, 'You and I are about to do something remarkably stupid.'

The firepower from the ERF side suddenly diminished; a moment later five smoke grenades were propelled forward through the hatch, followed closely by a massive barrage of bullets. A second later the barrage lifted whilst SC and Pillar leaped over the ERF soldiers holding position at the hatch and landed into the smoke before opening up fire all around them. Neither man was particularly sure of where they were so both took to the floor just in time to avoid the hail of bullets whizzing over their heads from their own team. Using the confusion and cover of the smoke, the two men looked quickly to discern their surroundings and find cover at the side of a console. However, they were still unsure of the whereabouts of the enemy soldiers.

The Fedirian soldiers fared no better as they were unable to fire their weapons with any real commitment or accuracy due to the smoke being slow to lift. As soon as the Command Centre's air conditioning was able to clear the smoke, the enemy was faced with fallen comrades all around them, confirming that the surprise push and hail of gun fire had found its mark on a number of targets. The fight was far from over as there were still half a dozen Fedirian troops held up in well covered positions, making entry through the open hatch for the attackers an impossibility; however, the cover wasn't good enough to stop the two ERF soldiers who had already infiltrated the defences. Immediately they were able to dispose of the three closest enemy troops, forcing the remaining three to lift their barrage on the hatch and attempt to hit the two interlopers. The effect of this action allowed ERF marines to storm the hatch, killing two of the three remaining defenders.

In a staggering move, the remaining Fedirian jumped across his console, firing his weapon and hitting SC in the shoulder and causing the Captain to drop to the deck like a ton of bricks. In his trauma he didn't see the creature cover the ground in a single step to grab hold of Pillar and pull a sharp blade out of a sheath strapped to his long leg. He held the weapon to the throat of the young soldier. For a moment the entire room was silent; the Marines held their position, weapons drawn, looking for the moment to take the shot and end the siege. However, their reluctance to fire was evident, as no one wanted to be responsible for the death of the amiable young Sergeant. The Fedirian shouted at the men surrounding him; however, no one present could discern what he was saying. The whole place was aware that time was running out; footsteps on metal decking could be heard down two of the three corridors approaching the Command Centre.

SC was close enough to the Fedirian to touch him, but from his injured position on the floor he couldn't do anything without instantly allowing the enemy troop to kill Pillar. Slowly the Captain looked around and caught sight of Amy, who was hiding out in the corridor out of sight of the Fedirian, looking as though she was working furiously on the door panel. Suddenly Amy turned around and noticed SC looking at her, causing her to smile nervously at him before slamming the button in front of her as hard as she could, which caused a loud wailing noise resounding through the Command Centre. The Fedirian, along with everyone else in the room, jumped in confusion. Thinking fast in all the confusion, SC swiped at Pillars legs as hard as he could causing, him to drop to the floor in pain but opening up the enemy to a hail of gunfire which ended him where he stood.

The footsteps from the corridor were almost on top of them, rushing towards the control console. Amy went straight to work, locking all of the blast doors around the Command Centre and sealing the ERF inside. 'Room is secure, Captain,' she said, 'what now?'

SC climbed back on to his feet, clutching his shoulder, 'Are the computer consoles still in working order?' The exhausted intelligence officer nodded to the Captain in confirmation.

Taking a moment to survey the room, and seeing the exasperated troops around him, SC could hear the banging on the doors as the enemy troops were trying to break through the blast doors. 'Vent the entire station with the exception of this room.'

'Sir? We have them contained, is that really necessary?' Responded the young officer.

'They wouldn't think twice about doing it to us Lieutenant; now vent the station.' SC replied, looking straight at her.

'But sir…'

'Amy!' The Captain shouted, 'Do it now!'

Amy looked around the room briefly, stopping at Pillar who gave her no support. Resolved to her task she looked at her console and opened all airlocks in the main body of the station. Moments later, the vacuum of space carried the remaining Fedirian soldiers to their death.

Amy looked up to find SC stood right behind her with his hand placed lightly on her shoulder, 'I know that was hard, but they were already dead, if we had blown up this station, or if they had been imprisoned, they would have been killed; you gave them a quick death.' Amy nodded her head, a small tear formed in her eye.

SC radioed Derek and let him know that the station was theirs and he could begin boarding some people. The team on board was carrying out a roving patrol around the station, on the lookout for possible survivors. The Eagles' Captain agreed to send down additional soldiers to help with the search.

Amy traced the files she needed to access, giving historical data, operational orders and tactical information; however, it was all protected information, 'To bypass it I need access to the computer core, which is two decks down. Once there I should be able to fool the computer into resetting the passcode information. The translation software that you guys developed is making this so much easier than it would have been if we were having to read this in their language.'

SC smiled and nodded, 'The tech guys did something right for a change. Hold up a second and I'll come with you.'

Amy and SC set off down the corridor toward the elevator that would take them below, checking in with Pillar first so he knew what they were doing before they went. 'Be careful guys, we have been through there but only the once.' the Marine Sergeant reported.

The elevator opened and the duo were faced with a vast computer casing that was roughly the size of a large detached house, seemingly running directly under the Command Centre and comprising this entire area of the station. 'Wow, impressive.' commented the Intelligence Officer.

Quickly Amy set off to work, leaving SC to walk around and take a look at the scale of the device, 'We will be deciphering the information out of this for years, I reckon.' stated the Captain.

Amy smiled in agreement before looking up toward SC to respond,. Instead, she adopted a look of horror, 'Look out!'

The Swan docked with the station, adding its security personnel to assist with securing the former enemy structure. Selina Laverty made her way to the Command Centre, seeing Pillar she smiled, 'Good to see you in one piece, Sergeant,' her face dropped a little, 'I was sorry to hear about Hill.' she continued.

'Thank you, Captain,. However, you know how he was; he had to be the first one in to any situation.'

Selina nodded in agreement putting, her hand the younger man's shoulder. 'Do you know where SC is? I thought he would be here.'

'He went with Rover down to the Computer core, although that was a little while ago. Let me try and get hold of him.'

The Fedirian had totally taken SC by surprise, and unfortunately Amy's warning came too late, with the large creature clobbering the Captain over the head and causing him to hit the floor for the second time that day, this time losing consciousness. Realising that certain death was imminent, the young intelligence officer sprang at the attacker. Using his superior strength he expected to incapacitate the slight girl without too much trouble; instead he was treated to a variety of dives and avoidance manoeuvres, making it difficult for him to lay a hand on her; meanwhile, she was able to hit him and dodge the counter, confusing and dis-orientating the larger creature.

'Very good!' he laughed at her, clearly impressed by the young woman's agility.

Taken aback, Amy found her feet a safe distance back from the attacker, 'How are you speaking English?'

The creature took a swing at the blonde, which she easily ducked whilst countering with a leg sweep, which caused the Fedirian to fall on his back. Slowly he got back up laughing again, 'You are good, I under-estimated you.'

Maintaining her defensive stance, Amy tried again to gain some answers, 'Your grasp of the English language is very good; tell me how you came to learn it.'

The Fedirian smiled at her again. It was the first time that Amy had ever really accepted these aliens as actual people in their own right, rather than just a mindless plague of creatures. 'I was the one who studied your planet long before my colleagues arrived, I was watching and learning everything your people did; in order to do that I had to learn the primary languages of your culture.'

The enemies' grasp of the language was incredible by any standard, leaving the intelligence officer in awe of her opponent. His language prowess combined with the knowledge that he had been studying them for some time made it apparent that he would be a useful asset if the ERF could capture him. The real challenge would be how to incapacitate the alien without killing him. Unfortunately, Amy didn't get the opportunity to work out that theory: as she was taking her time sizing him up and trying to find a weak spot, she didn't hear the second Fedirian soldier coming up behind her until it was too late. The young officer tried to turn and defend, but was struck down with the butt of the troopers weapon.

SC awoke to find himself being held up in the strong clutches of a large Fedirian soldier. He was confronted by his original attacker, 'Good ,you are awake. I wanted you to be conscious when I killed you.'

'Look who swallowed an Oxford English dictionary,' glibbed SC sarcastically, 'Although I believe the word you were looking for was interrogate, rather than kill.'

'I do so enjoy Earth humour; it was one of the hardest things about eradicating your race. We don't really have sarcasm in our culture, but the greater good means we all have to make sacrifices.'

'Don't look now, but I think you might have gotten a handle on this sarcasm thing, so how about we call it an even exchange and leave it there: you go on your way and leave us on ours.' replied the plucky Captain.

'I shouldn't think you will be getting off that easily, my friend.' responded SC's captor, 'You will have to pay for the lives you have taken today, so there will be no letting you off, no interrogation, just a long painful death, or at least as long as I have time to make it.'

SC considered the words of his opponent. 'So tell me, what have I done to deserve this special treatment, or is it that you just don't have any interest in gathering intelligence?'

The Fedirian's smile returned, 'You think I am stupid; I know that there is no way you would give up information without prolonged torture, but even if you would, the person who ordered my colleagues to death by venting them out into space doesn't deserve the opportunity to live.'

'Is that what this is about? If you think that's bad, you should see the amount of your people I have ordered to death through our overall attack. I must have killed tens if not hundreds of thousands of your people, so if you want a reason to kill me, make it more worthwhile than the few hundred on this station.'

'You find this funny, the murder of my people?' Glared the large Fedirian soldier.

'No I find this hypocritical; you and your people arrive at my home planet without warning and butcher millions of innocent lives in your surprise attack, giving us no real way of defending ourselves, and you have the nerve to lecture me about the deaths of a few hundred soldiers!' SC spat back with venom.

SC's captor nodded to his comrade holding the young Captain, causing the restraining Fedirian to tighten his grip. The pilot felt as though his arms were in a vice as it was impossible to move. Just then he saw the reason for the increased hold, which was a large Fedirian fist launching itself against his face. The severity of the punch almost caused SC to drop out of consciousness again, a condition that was halted by the impact of a second punch landing on his already swollen face. Changing tact, the aggressor grabbed hold of the injured Captains scorched shoulder, which was still awaiting medical attention, from the earlier blast. SC screamed loudly as the searing pain shot through him; he knew this was just the beginning of the assault, but there was no way to contain the effect of the pain.

The scream was loud enough to jar Amy from her unconsciousness, causing her to slowly come around. She quickly realised that the situation was not safe and made a point of not attracting any attention. The intelligence officer was lying just behind SC and his Fedirian restraint; she could see the predicament that her Captain was facing, but found herself a little powerless to help him. If it was only one of them then she may stand a chance, but with two she would need assistance, and looking at SC, it wasn't going to come from him.

The pain was becoming so intense that the ERF Captain could feel himself blacking out from the pressure. But then his captor would release the grip, allowing SC to recover marginally before retightening. The elevator started whirring with noise just behind the Fedirian soldier, 'Well it looks as though we may have company, so we will have to cut this short just at the good bit; that way we can be ready for your cohorts.' With that the attacker drew his dagger and raised it above his head for maximum drive, thrusting it downward. He was too slow to register Amy diving forward, grasping the dagger from the Fedirian restrainer's leg holster and stabbing the foot-soldier in the leg. The unexpected intrusion caused the soldier gripping SC to drop to the floor, releasing his grip on the Captain, causing the attacker to completely miss his mark and almost drive his dagger into his own comrade.

The injured Fedirian had rolled on top of SC and was attempting to strangle the life out of him, and with his injured shoulder the young Captain was doing all he could to fight off the attack. Amy was standing toe to toe once again with the head Fedirian, trading dagger blows with him. Mostly she was avoiding the tip of his blade, until a lucky swing sliced her forearm. Clutching it for a second, she attempted to draw back from the opponent, but sensing weakness he advanced, looking for the chance to end this fight.

Seconds later Selina emerged from the elevator, sidearm already drawn; observing the scene in front of her, she quickly fired off three rounds into the back of SC's attacker, killing him instantly and the body slumping over the fallen officer, trapping him to the ground. Turning her gun on the alien attacking the intelligence officer, she motioned to depress the trigger when Amy screamed, 'Stop, don't kill him, we need him.'

The Fedirian looked Amy square in the eyes. 'You will never take me alive!' Raising his dagger he lunged at Amy, his footsteps cut short after the crack of Selina's sidearm, her bullet flying straight into the Fedirian's knee, causing him to stumble to the ground, calling out in agony. Moving quickly, Amy stamped on the alien's hand, breaking his fingers and releasing his grip on the dagger. As soon as the weapon was free the intelligence officer kicked it to safety.

For a moment the two women just looked at each other with relief, before hearing SC's muffled voice, 'Is there any way you could help me out from under here?' Both women laughed, and whilst Selina kept a trained gun on the captive, Amy assisted SC out of his corpse prison. Hugging both Amy and Selina in turn, the new Captain expressed his thanks, knowing without the two of them he would have been dead for sure.

Chapter 16

The fleet celebrated the tremendous victory they had achieved over the Fedirians. For the first time in eighteen months, the feeling of freedom was in the air. Selina and the Swan led a mission to rescue the survivors that had remained on the Moon and return them to Earth, finding four hundred and twenty seven people alive and well, if also feeling some abandonment issues.

The Eagle and the Dreadnought touched down into the Mars hangar bay in order to receive some much needed repair work, whilst Vice Admiral Lewis and Captain Hatherly were transported to the Mars medical bay for some advanced treatment. The doctors seemed to think the prognosis was good.

The people of Earth came out of hiding; out of the rocks, the mountains, the bunkers and the submarines, all with the intention of rebuilding the world. A worldwide identification process was to be set up so that of the two and a half to three million human beings left alive could maybe find some family out there. It was suspected that there were still some Fedirian forces alive on the planet, but they were to be found and captured.

The Fedirian officer that Amy had captured on the space station, whose name it turned out was Garcosh, found himself awaiting a trial to answer for his peoples' attempted genocide. In the meantime, however, he was transported to a secure military facility to be interrogated, though he swore that he would tell them nothing.

A new world government was to be implemented, governing the entire planet instead of individual countries, hoping that a cut in bureaucracy would allow the remaining inhabitants of Earth to re-build a functional society with greater ease.

After some much needed medical treatment SC and Amy returned to the captured station with a technical team and set about unlocking the secrets held by the new space station, hoping to gain some insight into force strength in the area and attempt to find out why Earth was so popular in the first place. 'Captain, I think I've found it,' Amy shouted, pointing to her computer Screen, 'according to this, the Fedirian home world, Fedoria, is on the verge of destruction, they have estimated that their planet has less than ten years left. They have colonised lots of moons and expanded their civilisation across the galaxy; however, without a home world they have no place to belong. After observing and analysing human beings the Fedirians realised that we shared similar qualities and needs from an environment, which I'm guessing is why we have felt ok in their space ships and this station. So a decision was made that they would conqueror Earth and transform it into New Fedoria.'

'They had one hundred and fifty thousand troops on the ground down there before we bombed the hell out of it, is it safe to assume that wasn't the whole colony?' inquired SC.

'No sir, not even close. If I am reading this correctly, that was only the advance building team; they are still looking to move in. Sir, it looks as though the entire home world population are on their way here to begin their new life. I am detecting around one hundred thousand ships on a direct course for Earth.' answered the Lieutenant.

'One hundred thousand!' SC exclaimed, 'How long until they get here?'

'A little over three months!'

www.ingramcontent.com/pod-product-compliance
Lightning Source LLC
Chambersburg PA
CBHW020405150626
46554CB00012B/284